Sue Ellen finally accepted J.R.'s cruel rejections. Theirs would be a marriage in name only. There were many things that the Ewing money could buy but love wasn't one of them. Still, Sue Ellen dreamed she would someday have a baby—it was the only dream she had left.

_____

Series Story Editor *Mary Ann Cooper* is America's foremost soap opera expert. She writes the nationally syndicated column *Speaking of Soaps*, is a contributor to leading soap opera magazines, and has appeared as a guest on numerous radio and television talk shows.

Writers *Paul Mantel* and *Avery Hart* are, between them, the authors of plays, records, educational cassettes, and humor articles. They live in New York City, but have come to think of Dallas as their second home.

Dear Friend,

The character of J.R. Ewing has quickly become the classic example for today's successful villain. Even though J.R. does dastardly things, Dallas fans can't seem to get enough of the guy. Although it seems that J.R. never loses, he really does. You just think he always wins because he always manages to land on his feet.

In *Love's Challenge*, Book 3 of our DALLAS series, J.R. is in his finest form. And we discover the complexity of the Ewing family. There is nothing simple about the way any of them deal with each other.

Each volume of this Soaps & Serials series of books is taken directly from the original stories and scripts of DALLAS. Great care is taken that the stories and characters accurately reflect the show itself. So happy reading—it will be just as you remember it.

For Soaps & Serials Books,

Mary Ann Cooper

Mary Ann Cooper

P.S. If you missed Books 1 and 2 of this series, see the order form on page 192 which also tells you how to order books in our other Soaps & Serials™ paperback series.

DALLAS™

LOVE'S CHALLENGE

From the television series created by David Jacobs

Soaps & Serials™

PIONEER COMMUNICATIONS NETWORK, INC.

From the television series DALLAS™ created by David
Jacobs. This book is based on scripts written by Arthur
Bernard Lewis and Darlena Craviotto.

DALLAS™ paperback novels are published and
distributed by Pioneer Communications Network, Inc.

SOAPS & SERIALS™ is a trademark of Pioneer
Communications Network, Inc.

ISBN: 0-916217-83-3

Printed in the United States of America

10 9 8 7 6 5 4 3 2 1

LOVE'S
CHALLENGE

Chapter One

The scent of fresh-cut flowers filled the room where the Daughters of the Alamo were having their monthly meeting. Pamela Ewing was attending now as a special favor to her sister-in-law, Sue Ellen Ewing, head of the Library Benefit Committee. Sue Ellen, J.R.'s wife, had been asked to deliver the committee report and had asked Pam to come along. Since Pam had nothing else to do, she had agreed. But now she regretted it. The meeting was boring beyond belief and it seemed interminable as well! She was pleased that she had dropped out of this group and didn't have to attend regularly.

Sue Ellen was at the podium droning on about the benefit the Daughters were planning for the Dallas Library. How ironic, Pam thought, that a woman like Sue Ellen, who hadn't read a serious book in years, would be so involved in a library benefit. Pam smiled despite herself. Whatever she thought about Sue Ellen or the Daughters of the Alamo, she had to admit that the group did accomplish a number of good things for the community. If only the meetings weren't so long and uninteresting, and the members so ridiculously petty, she might have enjoyed participating herself.

Ever since she'd married Bobby Ewing, Pam had tried her best to fit into this wealthy community. Bobby had married her despite strong objections from his family, especially from his older brother, J.R., who disapproved of the match because Pam was a member of the rival Barnes clan. Pam's father, Digger Barnes, had been partners with Jock in the early wildcatting days of the Texas oil industry. He claimed that Jock had cheated him out of a vast fortune, a charge Jock vehemently denied. He contended that Digger had signed his part of their oil business away for a few cases of liquor.

Digger certainly did have a drinking problem and Jock seemed to enjoy taking advantage of it. Pam had once heard him brag to J.R. that Digger was an "ideal" partner because of his proclivity for drink and his willingness to sign away his assets. Maybe both men were telling the truth, thought Pam, but that was all in the past. Her marriage to Bobby represented an end to that feud (at least in her eyes and in Bobby's) and she was determined to take every step she could to make peace between the families.

After all, Pam thought, her attention drifting further and further away from Sue Ellen at the podium, she hadn't known Bobby was a Ewing the first time she saw him, and Bobby hadn't known she was a Barnes. But the love that had blossomed between them was stronger than a feud about things that happened over forty years ago. If only her brother Cliff, and Bobby's brother J.R. could accept each other, this feud would be effectively ended.

Because she had been a Barnes, it was imperative that Pam try to fit in with the way of life at Southfork. In addition to the usual nervousness a new bride might feel with her husband's family, Pam had carried the burden of her maiden name like a heavy weight. At first all the women had been so suspicious of her—except for Bobby's kind and wise mother, whom everyone called Miss Ellie.

Even young Lucy, though only a girl of sixteen, had treated Pam as if she might have been a spy the first couple months after Pam moved to Southfork. Now, the girl had taken a liking to Pam. Whatever the cause of the acceptance, Pam mused, she was grateful for Lucy's friendliness. As Jock and Ellie's only grandchild, Lucy's amiability was very welcome.

In order to gain Sue Ellen's acceptance, however, Pam had had to make bigger adjustments. She even went so far as to be initiated into the Daughters of the Alamo. Ewing women had a long history of membership in the Daughters going all the way back to great-grandmother Southworth, and it was an unwritten rule that modern Ewing women would participate as well.

When Pam chose to drop out of the club, she had been afraid that she would incur the wrath of Miss Ellie. But her new mother-in-law had been sweet and understanding about it, gracefully saying that Pam should do what she felt best and meaning every word. Like Pam, Miss Ellie had no interest in continuing the Barnes-Ewing feud. She was far too wise to want to see her family torn apart for any reason. Pam caught a glimpse of the older woman sitting at a table toward the front. Nodding at her warmly, she felt privileged to have such a gracious and understanding woman as her mother-in-law and friend.

Sue Ellen was certainly doing a first-rate job at the podium, Pam thought, turning her attention back to her sister-in-law. Pam wondered if Sue Ellen had once felt as she did—like an outsider who had to gain the Ewing family trust and acceptance inch by inch. If she had, it certainly didn't show now. Sue Ellen was the ideal of the modern Ewing woman: active in the community and a champion shopper. She sat at the dinner table every night looking adoringly at the husband who had betrayed her trust a thousand times. Even though J.R.'s philandering was well known around Dallas, Sue Ellen continued to act as if he were loyal and their marriage perfect. Was she an expert at covering her feelings—or didn't she care? Watching her deliver her address in a crisp black and white suit with a black brimmed hat, Pam heard only an almost imperceptible tremble in Sue Ellen's voice betraying her deep feelings of insecurity and embarrassment.

"The members of the committee suggest that it would be best to hold the event at the library, itself, after hours, of course," Sue Ellen said, smiling. "And we thought it would be in keeping with the mood to hire a chamber quartet to play some sort of light classical music in the background while Marilou Garr recites from Emily Dickenson, T.S. Eliot and other outstanding American literary figures. We also recommend a sparkling rosé wine and *petit fours* for refreshments, and single pink roses with baby's breath for decorations."

As Sue Ellen's planned remarks came to an end, she took on a noticeably vulnerable quality. Pam realized that no matter how cool her demeanor, Sue Ellen was a nervous wreck.

Turning her large brown eyes away from her audience ever so slightly, Sue Ellen said shyly, "Well, that's about it. I now open the floor for any comments or questions."

This was the part of the meetings that Pam found most enervating. A discussion would soon be underway that would take over an hour to make decisions about the simplest little issues. This meeting was going to be no exception.

A flurry of hands waved across the room as the members brought up their objections and suggested alternative ideas.

"Wouldn't a country band and chili be more suitable for this benefit?" asked Jane Ames, a portly Texan woman who, despite her vast city wealth, retained a country twang in her voice. "This is Dallas, after all. I can't see our husbands enjoying this event if they have to sit through chamber music and poetry readings and sip French wine!"

The room buzzed with insulted objections.

Speaking for the majority, a slender well-coifed woman attempted to lighten the proceedings and retorted, "Now, Jane, our husbands have come off the range—most of them, that is."

The group tittered at her comment as she sat down and a garishly-dressed matron stood up. "No offense to you, Sue Ellen, I personally think the committee did a wonderful job making its selections, but there are those of us who feel it would be more suitable to hire professional speakers for the poetry reading—perhaps some local actors. I'm sure Marilou would agree that a professional might be able to bring some meaning to a lot of old poetry that an amateur simply could not. No offense, Marilou."

Marilou Garr looked alternately hurt and angry. "The Daughters may not realize it, because I am not one to brag, but I have been a member of Actor's Equity since 1938 when I was hired to play the part of Miranda in a summer stock production of *The Tempest*!" she exclaimed. "And I would have pursued a career, too, if Willie Joe hadn't begged me not to and proposed to me that very summer!"

And so it went. Pam couldn't wait to leave this meeting. She restlessly shifted in her chair and consulted her watch. She would call Bobby and see if he could meet her for lunch as soon as she could break away.

The days were long when Bobby was at work. Before she married, Pam had been a busy, self-supporting woman—working, dating, keeping up her apartment, working out, seeing friends—but now, since she'd moved to Southfork, her life had become simpler and, in a way, duller.

It was ironic, Pam thought, that for once in her life she had all the material comforts a person could ever dream of—servants, financial security—yet she missed those days when she would come home from work exhausted, take a quick shower and go see a film with friends. It wasn't that she'd had any falling out with her old friends, it was just that her life had changed. Marrying a Ewing had put her in a new arena, and some of her old friends were uncomfortable with her now no matter how hard she tried to reassure them that she still needed them.

Now Pam's days stretched out in long spans of emptiness. She had tried to strike up a friendship with Sue Ellen, but the two were really cut from different cloth. Shopping, which was Sue Ellen's main pursuit, just wasn't enough, and the Daughters of the Alamo didn't meet her needs either. More and more Pam had come to rely on Bobby for companionship and stimulation. Maybe I lean on him too much, Pam thought reflectively. She was determined to catch any problems in her marriage and deal with them before they did any real damage.

The vote was finally over. White wine would replace the sparkling rosé, and beer would be available in case it was requested. A chamber quartet would be hired, and professional actors from the local regional theater would do the readings. Marilou Garr would introduce them all, including the mayor and the head librarian. As Sue Ellen banged her wooden gavel on the oak table standing next to her, the ladies applauded, and Pam wasted no time getting up and finding a phone.

It was a perfect day for herding cattle. The breeze swept across the open Texas range taking large puffs of white cloud with it. Only when the breeze stopped and the air was still, did someone feel the blazing sun baking the range and the creatures below.

The ranchers had a big job on their hands. Hundreds of head of cattle were being moved from the back six hundred acres to the corrals nearest the Ewing's estate, Southfork Ranch. It was hard work, and the cowboys were dusty and tired, their faces stained by rivers of sweat.

For most of the men, moving the cattle was just a job—something to tide them over until they rode in the next rodeo, or received a paycheck to send home. But for Jock Ewing, owner of Southfork and founder of Ewing Oil, the work meant much more.

After a life in the ruthless arena of the independent Texas oil industry, Jock found the work of the ranch exciting and invigorating. He no longer had a taste for the boardroom and the deal-making that went on there. It was the scent of the soil and the feel of a horse beneath him that he lived for now. Being out on the range, to him, was almost like being thrown back to another, more challenging time—when cattle was king, not oil, and a man made his way by working with the land, not by exploiting it.

Sweating profusely as he rode next to his ranch foreman, Ray Krebbs, Jock motioned that he'd like to stop for a moment. Settling himself under a shady grove of giant oak trees and smiling to himself despite his exhaustion, Jock pulled a pack of cigarettes from his shirt pocket and sighed deeply.

Hitting the package so that three or four cigarettes fell forward, he automatically offered a smoke to Ray, who wrinkled his face and shook his head negatively. He thought that smoking was like putting coffin nails in his mouth. When is Jock going to quit that stupid habit, Ray thought, more with concern than annoyance. Jock isn't getting any younger, and yet he abuses his health as if he were a young man, without thinking of the risks.

His chest still heaving from the hard ride, Jock felt in his pants pocket for the solid gold cigarette lighter that he always carried. It looked out of place, somehow, on the dusty beige range; it belonged in an executive suite, perhaps, or in an elegant restaurant. Looking at the lighter, the only clue that he was any different from the other cowboys driving cattle that day, Jock laughed to himself at the incongruity of its presence. Nevertheless, as he snapped the flame on with ease, he savored the feeling of the warm gold in his fingers. Jock was proud of the wealth he had amassed during his life, and since this was a symbol of that wealth, he was proud of it, too.

Jock inhaled the first breath of smoke. He knew he had to relax. He could feel his heart pounding hard inside his chest. Moving the cattle was work for the young and strong. And although he wanted to think he was both those things, the wild beating of his heart was telling him otherwise. Closing his eyes for a moment under the shade of the tree, Jock sighed with forced relief. But before his cigarette was half consumed, the squawk of Ray's walkie-talkie interrupted the peace of the moment. Jock regarded Ray carefully as the foreman put the instrument to his ear and listened with concentration. Ray took his work seriously, a fact that the Ewing patriarch appreciated deeply.

Turning to Jock as he replaced the walkie-talkie in his back pocket, the younger man said simply, "There's a little problem with a couple strays just south of here, Jock. I'll take care of it and be right back."

"Now, just a second, Ray," Jock responded, almost angrily, "I didn't come out here to sit around. I'll join you." And with that the old man dug in his heels and took off to the south, a trail of hot dusty soil clouding the air behind him.

Ray was concerned. Jock Ewing was his boss, and as an employee he had no right to interfere with Jock's wishes. But on the other hand, he was fond of Jock and it hurt to see the older man pushing himself beyond the limits of his endurance. Jock had been a businessman all his life, not a rancher. Ray could tell that riding the range on a hot day was too much for Jock. His face was flushed and he was breathing too hard. Now he even wanted to run after some strays. Ray shook his head in uneasy frustration before he rode south to join Jock and help him herd in the strays.

Galloping off about a half a mile, the men found the strays—about fifteen cattle who had stopped for a drink in the rushing creek that ran through the back acres of Southfork Ranch. As the men approached, it was clear the beasts had little intention of following orders and leaving the cool comfort of the creek. The ranchers knew that the only way to get the cattle away from water and shade on a hot day was out-and-out intimidation. Jock started yelling at the beasts. "Okay, that's enough!" he boomed. "Come on you! Let's get a move on! Let's go, you lazy bovines! Hustle!"

The power of his voice was undeniable, even for the animals. Raising their large eyes at him in bewilderment, the strays reluctantly began putting one hoof in front of the other until they were out of the creek bed and moving toward the rest of the herd on the range. It was easy to see that Jock Ewing was having the time of his life. When the animals were finally back with the main herd, Jock reached in his pocket for another smoke.

"You know, sometimes I think I should have been born back in the frontier days," he told Ray who stood nearby with a worried look on his face, watching the sweat fall off the older man's forehead.

As the sun penetrated his massive office windows, Bobby pored over the long-forgotten maps he found in the back of his file cabinet when he had first come to work at Ewing Oil. For over two months, he'd been trying to get J.R. to look at them. These forgotten landholdings were worth a fortune to the company if they could be properly developed. But J.R. never seemed to have time to discuss them. Bobby's frustration had grown to the extent that he was actually considering leaving Ewing Oil altogether—something he knew would hurt his father very much. That's why he was determined to give J.R. every possible chance to consult with him about the land. Leaving the family business would be a last resort, and if there were a way to avoid it, Bobby would try to find it.

This morning when Bobby had come into the office, he had immediately checked with J.R.'s secretary, Louella, to see if J.R. had any free time. Sure enough, the lunch hour was wide open. That's when Bobby planned to give it another try. He knew how much he had disappointed Pam. She'd sounded let down on the phone, but she understood how much it meant to Bobby to succeed at Ewing Oil. Now that he was married, he wanted to make his wife and family proud. His playboy days were over, and there was no better way to prove that than to succeed as the co-president of the company his father had founded. But that success required J.R.'s cooperation.

Looking at his watch, Bobby saw it was time to act. Without warning, he strode into his brother's office.

"J.R.—I'd like to make a review of Ewing's landholdings with you and it won't take much time. It seems to me that the land is just sitting there when it could be making the company a lot of money!"

J.R. sighed. He had heard all this before. Bobby seemed hell-bent on capitalizing on the worthless land that Jock had bought for a song back in the forties, in the hopes of finding more oil. But, as far as oil was concerned, these lands were drier than dust. J.R. would have sold them years ago except for the fact that the taxes on them were negligible and represented the kind of small deduction that the successful oil company needed. For forty years or so, the land was just an unused part of the company's assets. But that was completely appropriate in J.R.'s eyes—theirs was an oil business, after all, not a real estate firm.

"Now, Bobby, I know you have some cockamamie idea that those holdings are valuable, but I'm telling you there's not enough oil in them to make a jar of petroleum jelly."

Bobby sighed. J.R. seemed to have some sort of mental block about the landholdings. Once again he tried to explain his idea slowly and simply. This time J.R. *had* to understand. Bobby had been put off so many times about his idea he wasn't about to be brushed off again. He knew his idea was sound.

"J.R., I don't think you're listening. I know the land isn't profitable as far as oil is concerned, but what I'm trying to get across to you is that the property itself is ripe for development. A lot of this acreage was far away from civilization when Daddy bought it, but times have changed. Look at these . . ." he said, thrusting a map under J.R.'s nose. "Take this one parcel. Four hundred acres outside of Houston. Well, Houston was just a cowtown when Daddy bought this land, but now this parcel is prime real estate for development!"

J.R. gently pushed the map back to his brother. "Bobby," he said, apologetically, "I'd love to hear more, but I'm due at Harv's any minute. I'm still working on that Panhandle deal and I have to iron out a lot of details."

"Well, why don't I come along with you and we can talk on the way?" Bobby suggested, trying to mask his frustration. "Besides, I'd like to be there when you meet with Harv. I've been kind of in the dark on the whole Panhandle operation, and since Ewing Oil is so heavily involved, I think I should be there."

J.R. looked up at his little brother, surprised. He was being cool about it, but Bobby was issuing him a definite challenge. Just last week he had done something similar—barging into J.R.'s office for a so-called "frank talk." Bobby had been upset because J.R. had never included him in any of the important decisions at Ewing since he had joined the company months ago. J.R. had denied this and put him off as best as he could, and Bobby had left the meeting looking defeated, which was just fine with J.R.

The truth was that ever since Bobby had taken a position at Ewing Oil, J.R. had done everything in his power to keep his younger brother away from any real action. It had been understood by both of them, according to their father's wishes, that J.R. would train Bobby and break him in until he had the background to share the decision-making position with J.R. But J.R. didn't like to share power. Especially if he didn't have to. His idea from the very beginning had been to give Bobby a beautiful office and a secretary to match while he ran the company by himself.

As the firstborn, J.R. considered Ewing Oil to be *his* rightful heritage. As for Bobby, J.R. had always thought that with his looks and charm he should concentrate on being a playboy, not an executive. After all, Bobby had never before expressed any interest at all in Ewing Oil. But after he married that Barnes girl, she seemed to start pushing Bobby to take his work seriously. It was a distressing situation for J.R.—and one that had to be changed. Somehow J.R. would have to get rid of Pamela, or Bobby had to be forced out of Ewing Oil.

J.R. had tried luring Bobby away from his young bride by setting Bobby up with his oldest and hottest former flame, Jenna Wade, but that scheme had fallen through.

Now, Bobby had this new idea about the landholdings—admittedly brilliant—but *not* the kind of idea J.R. wanted Bobby espousing. Bobby's suggestions had to be crushed. Maybe then Bobby would take the hint that if he wanted "meaningful" work, he'd better look for it elsewhere.

J.R. looked up at his brother's waiting face. "I'm

sorry, Bob. Harv asked specifically that we meet alone. You know Harv. He's strange that way," he said, the picture of sincerity.

His plan was effective. Bobby looked defeated as he reluctantly rolled up his pile of maps.

"And about those landholdings, little brother, try me next week, okay?" J.R. said, patting his brother's shoulder reassuringly. He didn't add: "I won't be available then either," but he thought it.

Chapter Two

After dinner with the family at Southfork, Sue Ellen and J.R. made their way up the mansion stairs to their private quarters. J.R. usually spent the evening reading financial reports, while Sue Ellen turned her attention to television or to crossword puzzles. When J.R. would look up from the page, he'd often see Sue Ellen smiling at him uncomfortably, as if she wanted to say something, but when he returned the smile and waited for her to speak, she said nothing and J.R. went back to his papers. The wealthy and attractive Mr. and Mrs. J.R. Ewing rarely talked, and they made love even less.

Sue Ellen had tried many ways, over the years, of getting J.R. to talk about his activities at work, but her husband had steadfastly refused to tell her anything about his life at the office. When she used to ask him about Ewing Oil, it hadn't been out of an interest in the company but out of a desire to be more involved with her husband.

But no matter how often she tried, J.R. had

always responded the same: "Now, honey," he'd say with a tired look on his face, "why do you want to fill up your pretty little head with a bunch of facts and figures about business?" His message had always been clear—"Leave me alone."

After a few years of meeting such resistance she'd tried interesting him in her activities. At first, he feigned interest, but soon after, when she began telling him about a meeting of the Daughters or a shopping excursion she had, he showed his boredom all too clearly. He'd nodded his head perfunctorily and even yawned.

Sue Ellen's last resort had been sex. Without being bold or aggressive, she would leave little hints around their rooms that would let him know she would be receptive to his approach—a black lace teddy draped a chair, a pair of silk panties hung in the bathroom. But even then, J.R. had always seemed more interested in his mysterious late-night appointments in Dallas than in his wife of seven years.

Still, there had to be a way. Unbeknownst to anyone in the Ewing family, Sue Ellen had even consulted the library looking for books on improving marriage through sex. This topic had become an obsession with her—for if they had a more active sex life, she and J.R. would have a better chance of conceiving a child.

In the past, she had been ambivalent about having a baby, mostly because she dreaded the thought of losing her beauty contest figure and being up all night meeting the needs of a tiny infant. But, according to her husband's wishes, she had never used any kind of contraception to avoid getting pregnant. J.R. said he wanted to provide Jock with a grandson as soon as they could. Sue Ellen, a cooperative, obedient wife, had agreed to let nature take its course. There was a small part of her that was proud that her husband wanted her to be the mother of his children —though secretly, she thought it would be nice to wait for a few years.

In those early years, each month she realized she was not pregnant was a cause for private celebration for Sue Ellen. But after several years had gone by, her relief had changed to worry. What if something were wrong with her or with J.R.?

To quiet her fears, she had a complete fertility workup with the best specialist in Dallas. She checked out completely normal. But J.R. had refused to go for any sort of testing. He had seemed to take the idea as some kind of affront to his manhood and had hardly spoken to her for weeks after she suggested he look into the matter. He assured her that he knew in his heart he was a "normal, red-blooded American boy," and that was that; this issue was closed. Just as with every other matter of importance in their marriage they couldn't communicate about this.

Having a child had become vital to Sue Ellen— the answer to all her marital problems. A child would draw her husband closer to her—she was sure of it. If they had a child, J.R. would have to pay more attention to her. And more than that, she would have something to do with her time. But best of all, as the mother of a Ewing scion, she would be honored by her in-laws and respected by her husband. Now she was like a useless appendage, she thought bitterly—a pretty accessory on J.R.'s

24

arm when he wanted her—but one that he could just as easily forget about when he didn't. Before there could be a child, there had to be sex. Looking across the room at her husband, she strengthened her determination to seduce him.

J.R. sat in the tall leather chair by the fireplace, the reading glasses he wore only in the privacy of his own rooms balanced on his nose, as he consulted the back pages of the *Wall Street Journal*.

Walking up to him from behind, her silk blouse unbuttoned to reveal the curve of her breasts, Sue Ellen tenderly placed her hands on his shoulders. There was no response. Having read just that afternoon in one of the books she kept hidden in her lingerie drawer that men adored it when their wives took a bold approach to sex, she leaned into the chair and wrapped her arms around her husband's neck, then began nuzzling his ear with her full soft lips.

"Stop it, honey," he said unfazed. "I'm reading."

Another night Sue Ellen would have taken him at his word and walked into the other room and cried. Tonight, she disregarded his reproach and became even bolder. The book had said to overwhelm your man with sensuality, ignore his protests, and move in like a lioness.

"That's enough reading!" she said, gently taking the paper from his hands and easing herself over the arm of his chair until she was on his lap with her arms around him, her fingers busy undoing the buttons on his shirt. Then, when her hands reached under the cloth and began to stroke his chest, she whispered throatily, "I want you, J.R. Now."

J.R. didn't know what had gotten into his wife.

Sue Ellen was acting like a common floozie, and if there was anything that turned him off it was a woman who was cheap and obvious. A professional would never act like Sue Ellen was acting now. That's why J.R. liked dealing with professionals. In fact, he had an appointment with one later in the evening, and sex with Sue Ellen now would simply be diverting

But not wishing to offend her, J.R. looked up and smiled wearily, "Honey—I want to get this read before my meeting tonight. I have to present some of these figures to a man from New York."

It wasn't too bad a lie, he thought, with some amusement. Laurie's new girl had told him she once worked for a stockbroker in New York, until she found Laurie and an easy way to triple her salary by doing what she liked to do.

J.R. took his wife's hand firmly and gently pushed it away as he rebuttoned his shirt. "You know how much I'd like to make love to you, honey, but it's just not a good time," he said to placate her.

Secretly, J.R. was delighted that his wife seemed so eager. It was a sign to him that he was a sexually desirable man. Tonight, he would prove that prowess to the new girl at Laurie's house and enjoy every minute of it. There he would be uninhibited, and he could work off all the tensions of the day. Bobby was getting mighty cocky at Ewing Oil and J.R. knew a showdown was coming. He had to assert his authority at work in a way that would make Bobby back down for good. Tonight would help him relax so that he would be feeling refreshed and strong in the morning.

Looking at Sue Ellen J.R. smiled appreciatively.

He had married the prettiest girl in Texas and she had made a darling wife. Even tonight, without knowing what she was doing, she had helped him get the night off to a good start, he thought ironically. But the kind of sex he craved would be impossible with Sue Ellen, anyway. She wouldn't understand. Laurie's new girl didn't have to understand—she was paid to cooperate, not think.

Sue Ellen stood shakily and walked to the privacy of her bathroom as she had so many times before when she felt the hot sting of J.R.'s rejection. Looking into the mirror, she cried. How could they ever expect to have a baby if J.R. wouldn't even look at her?

It was after midnight when Ellie turned over in her sleep and automatically reached out for the reassuring touch of her husband. But instead of feeling his warm, solid flesh, her fingers fell on the sterile percale of the sheet. Her eyes still shut, she reached farther thinking he must have turned to the outside edge of the mattress. Still, she felt nothing.

Ellie sat up in bed and reached for the light switch of her bedside lamp. Jock was gone. Instinct told her something was wrong. He had been alternately tired and restless the past few months, throwing himself into the physical work of ranching with a passion far exceeding natural enthusiasm or pleasure. It was almost as if he were trying to drive the devil away. Even his digestion was giving him problems. Jock was a big man and had always been a big eater, but lately, after he consumed one of his regular meals, he would retire to his room complaining of heartburn.

When Ellie had insisted they call Dr. Danvers about it, Jock had pooh-poohed her, asserting vehemently that he felt just fine. But he couldn't hide the truth from the eyes of his observant wife. Forty years together was enough time for Ellie to know when her husband was well and when he wasn't. So, over her husband's objections, she had made an appointment for him with the doctor.

Dr. Danvers had given Jock a complete physical and had instructed him to make some vital changes in his life style unless he wanted to be the victim of a serious heart attack. He would have to change his diet and his eating habits completely, the doctor had said. He was to stop smoking immediately, cut down on fats and alcohol, exercise moderately, and above all, avoid stress like the plague.

After that visit to Danvers, Ellie had instructed the cooks to change the menu at Southfork and told Jock she would not tolerate his smoking any more. To placate her, Jock had thrown away his cigarettes, but when the urge to smoke hit him full-force the next day, he had secretly purchased a pack from a ranch hand and then kept them hidden out in the stables. One of the reasons he was so insistent about getting work done on the ranch was that it offered him a way to escape Ellie's all-seeing eyes. None of the ranch hands knew a thing about his visit to the doctor, and even if they had, they were in no position to reprimand him about his bad habits. No matter what they felt about him, Jock was still the boss.

Ellie stood up, reached for the thick velvet robe that she had hung over the back of the chair next to her bed, and started down the mansion steps. She thought she had heard the kitchen door shut as if someone had walked in from outside. Could it have been Jock? Whatever would he be doing out on the grounds at 2:30 in the morning?

As she swung open the kitchen door, she saw Jock, smoke spiraling from the cigarette he held in his fingers, opening the refrigerator to take out a gallon package of chocolate ice cream.

"Jock!" Ellie said, shocked.

Her husband spun around, caught in the act, trying to keep the cigarette out of Ellie's view.

"Why, Ellie. What are you doing up at this ungodly hour?" Jock asked aggressively, trying to turn the attention away from himself.

Despite herself, Ellie had to laugh. "What are *you* doing up is the question! I was looking for you!"

As she spoke, Jock had unobtrusively dropped the cigarette on the floor and crushed it out with the toe of his leather slipper. Owing to the lateness of the hour, he had hoped his wife's keen powers of observation were not fully operating. But he was wrong. Ellie walked passed him and picked the butt off the floor.

"Teresa won't appreciate cigarette butts on the floor, Jock," she said gently.

Jock shook his head in frustration as he went to the utensil drawer and picked out an ice cream scoop and began scooping a giant-sized portion of ice cream into a waiting bowl. Shrugging his shoulders in defiance of her disapproving look, he asked, "Want some, Ellie?" Without waiting for her answer, he took a huge spoonful and slowly brought it to his mouth, his eyes on her all the time.

For a moment, Ellie considered grabbing the

spoon from his hand and slapping his wrist as if he were a naughty boy. But this was her husband and he was not to be treated like a child. Obviously something was wrong or he wouldn't be acting so strangely. Jock was usually a sensible man, and the kind of behavior he was demonstrating now was a sure sign that he was troubled about something.

Joining him at the table, Ellie asked gently, "What's wrong, Jock? You can tell me."

"Oh, I couldn't sleep, that's all."

Ellie was silent. Experience had taught her that if she waited, he would soon share the thoughts that were upsetting him. But if she pried, he was apt to clam up.

"It's the boys," he said finally. "I had thought once Bobby joined the company I could rest and enjoy my retirement, but something is wrong at Ewing Oil. I can tell. Remember how eager Bobby was to get to work for the company a few months back?"

Ellie nodded. Bobby's enthusiasm for taking a position at Ewing Oil just a few months ago had been remarkable. He'd read up on the oil industry and talked to Jock for hours about how he might best participate in the company. Jock and Ellie were surprised because as a boy he'd never shown much interest in business. But after his marriage he was raring to go.

Jock's eyes betrayed the deep distress he was feeling. "Well, that's all changed, Ellie. He seems beaten down somehow."

Ellie said nothing, but her manner exuded a caring warmth that urged Jock to tell her more.

"Tonight, Ellie, at supper, when I asked Bobby

how things were going at work, he just sat there looking at his napkin while J.R. took over and gave me the whole run down. And every time I asked about details, it was J.R. who answered, even though I was looking straight at Bobby. I could feel the tension between them, too. You can almost cut it with a knife."

Having promised Ellie that he would not get involved in the day-to-day hassles of doing business at Ewing Oil, Jock had been all the more eager to hear about the goings on in downtown Dallas from his sons when they returned home from the office. With J.R. and Bobby at the helm, Jock had thought he would be able to get vicarious pleasure from his lifelong habit of dealmaking.

That's why, when Bobby had joined the company, Jock had felt so complete. Bobby's desire to be a success at the family business had made Jock a happy man. It was the crowning success of his fatherhood and the comfort of his retirement.

Jock had sired three sons—J.R., Gary, and Bobby. Gary just hadn't been cut out for business, or much else worthwhile, in Jock's opinion, and father and son had locked horns so frequently and so brutally that Gary had finally left Southfork for good. His departure broke Ellie's heart, but it had to be. And any plans Jock had for having Gary in the business were long dead.

As for J.R., his qualities of leadership had been proven to Jock many times. In the three years since Jock had retired—at Ellie's insistence—J.R. had been a complete success at Ewing Oil and Jock had generally been extremely pleased with his leadership. With J.R. at the helm, Ewing Oil would someday be the biggest independent oil company in the state of Texas. That was J.R.'s goal and he was driving toward it with full steam.

But J.R. had one problem. He was a fine businessman, as crafty and shrewd as any Jock had ever encountered in his day, but he had a way of grating on people, too. More than once, Jock had had to go to Dallas to smooth some feathers that his eldest son had ruffled. And as much as Jock loved his eldest son, he knew J.R. had a reputation for ruthlessness in business—a reputation that hindered the progress of Ewing Oil in subtle but definite ways.

Bobby, on the other hand, was by nature a gentle and sensitive man—he had natural charm, a keen intelligence, and a way of respecting others that made him the perfect partner for J.R. With Bobby in place, there was no way Ewing Oil wouldn't reach its maximum potential. Bobby and J.R. represented the ideal team to run Ewing Oil.

Jock had let the ice cream melt in its bowl as he stared ahead, tired and a worried man. Ellie took the bowl and placed it in the sink, then turned to her husband and took him by the hand.

"The boys will just have to work it out between themselves, Jock. They're full-grown men now and we shouldn't interfere. You don't need the stress, and they don't need a doting father."

Jock knew in his heart that she was right, but still, the whole situation hurt him badly. Letting himself be led back to their bedroom, Jock whispered, "I'll stay out of it, Ellie. I promise." And at the time he meant every word.

Chapter Three

Bobby sensed Jock was not feeling up to par as he watched him saddle up with Ray. But Bobby had to talk to his father right away. In an hour he would be heading for Houston in the family helicopter, embarking on a new adventure that would require Jock's support and understanding.

The night before, Bobby had spent hours thinking about his position at Ewing Oil and about the landholdings he had discovered. At about ten o'clock, he had put in a phone call to an old college buddy, Rory George, who, in the few years since their graduation, had become one of the state's biggest real estate developers. If his idea of forming a construction firm to develop the properties had any merit at all, Bobby could count on Rory to help him get a good plan together. Conversely, if the idea was off the mark, Rory would be honest about that, too.

Rory was the perfect man to consult with, but as Bobby had started laying out the plan and the problems, the two men realized that there was just too much to discuss in a simple phone call. That's why, Rory had suggested that Bobby fly down to Houston where they could really study the construction idea for a few days. Also, Rory was anxious to show off his new baby, Amanda, only three months old, but apparently already "incredibly gifted intellectually and musically."

Bobby had agreed to make the trip, telling Pam enthusiastically about his idea and why he needed to go to Houston. As usual, she had been his best supporter, urging him to research his idea thoroughly, letting him know in no uncertain terms that her gut reaction was that the plan—and Bobby—were brilliant.

Traveling to Houston on a day when he should theoretically be at work in the Ewing Building was a slap in the face to J.R. Bobby knew that, but he also knew that for his own survival, he had to take a cold, hard attitude toward J.R. Over and over, he told himself he didn't care about J.R. or his reaction. It wasn't true, and he knew it, but Bobby hoped that the sheer repetition would serve to convince him.

His father's feelings were an entirely different matter, however. Before Bobby left, it was essential to tell Jock his plans. Jock was an oil man from way back and was likely to balk at the construction idea, but it was only fair that he know what Bobby was up to. Maybe he would even embrace the idea openmindedly. That would be terrific, Bobby thought, but it was unlikely. More probably, Jock would resist at first until he had a chance to see the numbers on paper. Then, hopefully, he would give his blessing to Bobby's idea, and Bobby would never have to work with J.R. again.

His small leather overnight case tucked under one arm, Bobby steeled himself and walked through the huge wooden doors of the stable. Ray Krebbs waved and smiled at the youngest Ewing brother when he saw him walk in.

Of all the Ewing boys, Bobby was the one Ray was most fond of. Bobby was down-to-earth. He had good sense and he didn't let his Ewing name get in the way of his humanity. Gary had been so emotionally troubled, even as a boy, that Ray had never really been able to get to know him. As for J.R., all of Dallas knew the man was impossible. To J.R., the Ewing name made him better than other people and he did a poor job of hiding his contempt for the other members of the human race.

Ray motioned Bobby aside before the Ewing son had had a chance to call out his greeting to Jock. The foreman had been looking for an opportunity to talk to someone in the family about Jock and this was his chance. He had noticed that Jock's complexion was taking on an ashen hue after he did hard physical labor, and it alarmed the foreman who whispered casually, to hide the worry in his tone, ''Your father's been pushing it lately, Bobby. See if you can talk some sense into him.''

Bobby nodded as Jock looked up and said, ''I may be getting older, Ray, but I still have good ears! You just forget about me 'pushing it' and I'll forget you've been telling tales out of school to my son.'' Jock laughed, masking his fatigue and worry, and threw his arm around Bobby's shoulders.

''What's up, son? I know you wouldn't be here in the middle of a working day with that look on your face if something wasn't the matter.''

Bobby smiled. Nothing got past Jock. The elder Ewing had a well-known reputation as a sharp-eyed, keen observer of his friends and adversaries—a reputation that had won him many a battle in the business world and had made him an exceptionally perceptive father.

"Daddy—I'm leaving for Houston for a couple of days and I wanted to let you know why," Bobby explained with a hint of nervous breathlessness in his voice.

The older man looked shocked, but said nothing. In the silence, Bobby launched into a brief report of his findings of the Ewing land and his idea for beginning an independent construction company.

Jock studied his son, who was explaining his ideas with the same eagerness he once had for coming to work at Ewing Oil. A jolt went through the older man's body. The situation between his sons was far worse than he had even suspected. Bobby's beginning a company of his own was unthinkable, but something—or someone—had to be driving him pretty hard for him even to consider such a crazy idea. Jock interrupted. "It's J.R., isn't it, son? He's trying to restrain you at Ewing Oil, so you came up with this little scheme so that you'd have something for your own. Am I right, Bobby?"

There was no point in denying the truth. "I can't work with J.R., Daddy. I just can't. He's been the sole power at Ewing Oil for too long now, and he's just not willing to include me in anything important that goes on there. I feel like I'm an errand boy, and no matter how I've tried I can't seem to make a dent in the wall J.R. has put around the company."

Bobby's answer was confirmation of what Jock

thought might be happening. But the solution wasn't for Bobby to start a separate construction company! What did an oil baron know about construction, Jock thought. And like it or not, that's what Bobby was! Jock Ewing had prided himself on building an oil business from the dirt up—and he built it for his sons! Anybody could become involved in construction, Jock believed, but oil took special genius, genius that Jock was sure Bobby had as his birthright!

"Bobby, have you had a good old talk with J.R.?" Jock wanted to know, hoping the whole problem could be cleared up with a frank discussion. When he was a young man in business he was almost always able to eliminate problems by facing them right on. His ability to cut through difficulties with straight talk was legendary in Dallas. And it had worked with everyone—except Digger Barnes.

"You know, son, with J.R. you have to stand up for yourself. Your brother isn't the type to hand over the reins of the company, even share them, without a fight. That's why he's good at what he does."

Bobby felt completely drained. Jock just didn't comprehend the extent of J.R.'s refusal to share the company with him—and if Jock knew the hard facts, he'd probably deny them. Just a few months ago, J.R. had actually tried to break up Bobby's marriage and actually cause his and Pam's divorce in the hopes of getting him out of Ewing. The man had no limits to what he'd try if his territory was threatened. And it had become clear over the past months that he viewed Bobby's arrival at Ewing Oil as a very dangerous threat to that territory. There was no way he would ever gracefully relinquish some power to his younger brother.

Trying as best he could to explain the hopelessness of the situation without putting J.R. down, Bobby told his father the truth as he saw it.

"Daddy—I *have* stood up for myself, and it's done no good. J.R. keeps me away from any important meeting and, no matter what I say about it, he has some sort of reason why I can't go. And I can't work like that. Anyway, Daddy. I want to build and be productive with my work time—I don't want to have to be fighting someone all the time just so I can do my job. You can understand that, can't you?"

Jock understood perfectly. As he realized the true extent of the problem for the first time, a purple flush covered his face. The Ewing patriarch was enraged. How dare J.R. keep Bobby at bay like that—didn't he realize that Bobby was family—and family was sacred?

Most people would have found Bobby a pleasure to work with. He had brains, charm, and a fine sense of humor. What else did J.R. want in a working partner? It was clear to Jock that J.R. was totally at fault in this case, and he silently vowed to give his eldest son a thorough talking-to so that this mean business would end and the business at Ewing Oil could go forward—with Bobby in place!

Not wanting to show the extent of his feelings to Bobby, the older man simply sighed. "Okay, son. You go to Houston. Not that I approve, mind you. I don't. As far as I'm concerned the construction business is just so many hammers and nails, and I don't like the sound of anything I'm hearing. But you're a grown man and I'm not going to stop you."

That was as much of a blessing as Bobby had

expected from his father. Throwing his arm around the older man, Bobby gave him a quick squeeze and then muttered gratefully, "Thanks, Daddy," before he broke away toward the waiting helicopter. The pain of having to disappoint his father was behind him, and the excitement of a whole new project confronted him.

The sun burned down hard as Jock watched his youngest son walk away from him. He had done his best to calmly reassure Bobby, but his own feelings were grim and angry. Jock stood motionless until Bobby was lifted up into the sky. Then he called to one of the ranch hands to unsaddle his horse as he strode in the direction of the family mansion with steely determination.

J.R. was dressed in a hand-tailored suit as he sat on the porch, a pitcher of tomato juice on the table beside him. His cool fingers pressed his eye lids to help relieve their burning feeling from a long night spent in a smokey room. Every motion that he made, however slight, produced a colossal thundering in his aching head. This is surely one hell of a hangover, he thought. But his experience last night at Laurie's had been well worth it.

J.R. made out the figure of his father across the lawn, striding up to the house in his cowboy clothing. Why his father liked to wear plaid shirts and play with livestock was beyond J.R. but he supposed Jock had earned the right to do whatever he pleased in his later years—even if that right included making a damned fool out of himself. To J.R., there was nothing more to ranching than the smell of hay and dung—two odors he could happily live without for the rest of his life. Give him the boardroom, the smell of perfume, and a shot of bourbon any day.

"Mornin', Daddy," he said, mustering as much cheer as he could. No matter what little judgments J.R. might have about his father, he never forgot that Jock Ewing *was* Ewing Oil. Everything he had in life he owed to his daddy, and he knew it.

"J.R.," was the curt reply as the elder Ewing strode onto the porch. "Shouldn't you be at the office? Or are you running my company from here?"

J.R. was unruffled. Obviously, his father had some kind of grudge against the world this morning and J.R. wasn't about to take it personally. "Everything is under control, Daddy. It's just that I was out late last night, and I'm afraid I'm suffering the effects of a little too much alcohol."

Jock had often wondered, like everyone else at Soutfork, whom J.R. met with late at night. But his son was beyond the age when he felt he could pry into his personal affairs. J.R. always explained these late nights as business meetings, usually with people from out of state, implying that all businessmen kept such late hours nowadays. But Jock had never bought it. And J.R. was too smart a businessman to incur a hangover in the course of a meeting. No, his son's explanation just didn't wash.

Almost as if reading his father's mind, J.R. embellished his story. "It's the Panhandle deal I'm into with Willie Joe Garr and Jeb Ames. Those boys certainly can drink. And since they're financing us on the entire operation, I figure the least I can do is keep up with them."

J.R. was trying to be light. His story was a

fabrication from start to finish but one that he thought his father would appreciate. He was wrong. Jock wasn't in a mood to appreciate his eldest son's charm one little bit that morning.

"J.R.—what's going on between you and your brother? I want the truth now, hear?"

The question seemed to take J.R. by surprise. "Everything is just fine between us, Daddy. He's coming along real well, I'd say."

"Oh? You would? Well, I just had a talk with Bobby, and I gather from his point of view things aren't so fine. From what I can make out, you're treating him like some kind of junior trainee when his rightful position is co-president of the whole damned company!" The vein on the side of Jock's head was throbbing angrily.

J.R. did his best to turn the situation around. "I don't see why he came to you to complain. He never came to me."

"Well, according to him he has, many times! And you shut him out so thoroughly that he wants to get out of Ewing Oil and into some damned construction business!"

J.R. looked hurt and confused. He knew that an injured and bewildered response was the one Jock would most respond to in a moment like this. But inside, the news that Bobby was considering leaving Ewing Oil was the best news he'd heard all day. Suddenly, his headache was gone and the burning in his eyes had ceased.

Jock's voice continued booming. "I was very clear with you, J.R.! I told you to show Bobby the ropes so that the *two* of you could run the company *together*! I made my wishes very clear about that, didn't I? I know you understood my intention."

"Daddy", J.R. countered as humbly as he could, "Just as soon as he has a little experience I plan to bring him in on everything."

Jock was at the limit of his tolerance. "How long were you planning to take, J.R.? Five years? Fifteen? Ewing Oil is a family business and Bobby is your brother, damn it! He has the right to be in on every executive decision from the very start!"

"But, Daddy, "J.R. replied earnestly, "He's still a kid! He's not ready for that kind of responsibility!"

Jock was shouting now. "He's not a kid, damn it, and I want him included in on everything Ewing Oil is involved with! I want him to have a say in who you pick as the damned paperclip supplier and be at every meeting you have with the governor of the damned state—and everything in between! Everything! Get it?"

J.R. turned away from his raving father. He had to stay cool. He had to stay calm. But he also had to set his daddy straight about a few things.

"You asked me to run the company, Daddy," he said, gently, looking far off out onto the lawn where Miguel stood watering his mother's roses, "and I have to be able to do it as I see fit."

Then, turning to his father for emphasis, he was seized with panic. Jock was doubled over, unable to move, his eyes wide open in pain, the muffle of a scream in his mouth.

"Daddy! Daddy!" J.R. cried, bending over to help his father. But Jock could not speak. A searing pain, like a hot knife and struck through his heart had him in its burning clutches. He was beyond the simplest words.

Running into the house, J.R. called out to anyone who might hear him—the servants, Raoul, Ray Krebbs—anyone. But the house was empty. Breathless, J.R. raced back to the porch, picked up the telephone and pushed the button for the operator with his shaking finger.

"Get me an ambulance!" he shouted into the phone, his voice a raw command. "I want it right away! Right away! At Southfork Ranch. Someone has just collapsed!"

J.R. hung up and dropped to the ground so he could hold his father in his trembling arms until help arrived. Panting in fear, biting down hard on his lip, he could only sob, "Daddy, Daddy . . ." over and over again until he heard the thin whine of the ambulance begin its long journey to the entrance of Southfork.

Chapter Four

Ellie sat in the hospital waiting room. A magazine spread open, unread, lay on her lap. As nurses and aides walked up and down the well lit, light green corridors, her eyes searched anxiously for a sign of Harlan Danvers, the Ewing family physician. Jock had been in the Intensive Care Unit for over an hour, the victim of a massive heart attack. At that very moment, a team of doctors who were strangers to her were struggling to save his life, and there was nothing his wife could do but wait.

Whether her husband would live or die, she did not know. He was alive when he was first brought into the hospital, but his breathing had been faint—very faint. Now, he lay inside the area that was restricted even to loved ones and members of the immediate family. Only hospital personnel and the clergy were allowed through the white doors into the place where men and machines worked like demons to keep people alive.

Ellie's weary blue eyes closed in a silent prayer.

There were times when all one could do was to appeal to a higher power. This was such a time. "Give him strength. Give me strength and please, please, dear God, let him live!" Ellie prayed, over and over.

The circular clock on the hospital wall moved forward in agonizingly slow motion. Ellie opened her eyes again to search for Dr. Danvers. But the door of the intensive care unit stood silently still, separating Ellie from any information about Jock's condition.

Standing to stretch her legs Ellie couldn't help but worry. Was her hurried breakfast with Jock that morning going to be her final memory of the man she had lived with and loved for almost forty years? Why hadn't she told him how very much she had always loved him instead of grumpily complaining when he had helped himself to a second portion of bacon! Was his last image of her to be an unsmiling, irritated woman denying him even the simplest little pleasure?

Mixed in with her painful emotions was a hidden feeling of anger. Hadn't Jock been warned about the risk he was taking with his reckless life-style? Why had he chosen to ignore those warnings and put his life in jeopardy? Didn't he realize that by harming himself he was putting his wife in danger of having to live the rest of her life as a widow—a lonely widow—because there would never be another man for her but Jock Ewing. The first time she had set eyes on him as a youth of just twenty-two, she had felt a shiver go through her. Jock was the only man she had ever been with, the only man who ever knew the closeness of her body—the only man she could ever allow herself to love in that way.

J.R. paced nervously up and down the small waiting area, as he had been doing for two solid hours. Sue Ellen sat calmly working on her needlepoint, her feelings a blur of embarrassment and relief. When she had first heard the news from the Ewing butler, Raoul, he had said, in a panic-stricken voice, only that Mr. Ewing had collapsed. Sue Ellen had thought he meant J.R., as she rushed to her car and headed for Dallas Memorial Hospital. She had even embarrassed herself when she first saw her husband standing next to his distraught mother by saying, "J.R.! Thank God! I thought it was you!" How could she have been so insensitive, Sue Ellen wondered, ashamed of her brazen relief when she saw her husband alive and well.

But worse was J.R.'s whispered response, when Ellie was out of earshot. "I bet you were very disappointed."

How could he say such a vicious thing? Didn't he realize that despite all their problems, Sue Ellen loved him deeply? Hadn't she shown him her love repeatedly only to have him trample on it as he had the night before? Or was he merely joking? That's what he would tell her if she pressed him for an explanation. After seven years of marriage, J.R. still remained a mystery to her.

"Honey, sit down or you'll wear out the floor," Sue Ellen said gently to her distraught husband who finally slumped down next to her as if it were he who was sick and not his father.

At last, Dr. Danvers' white head appeared. Referring to his notes before he spoke, Ellie couldn't help noticing that the usually jocular doctor had a look of dead seriousness on his face. The news he was delivering could not be good news. It wasn't.

"Well, Ellie, his blood pressure is stabilized," the doctor reported. "But it's serious. Very serious."

J.R. jumped to his feet. One thing he hated was being at the mercy of someone else, even of health professionals, as he felt he and his mother were now. Turning to the doctor, he demanded in an authoritative voice, "Now, look here, Harlan—we want some answers and we want them now! What the hell is going on here? What's wrong with my Daddy, and how damned long is it going to be until you can fix it?"

Ellie turned to her son with reproach. "J.R.!" she said, chastising him. "I'm sure Harlan was just about to explain everything. Now, why don't you just have a seat while I talk to him—alone. In fact, after Harlan and I talk, I'd like you to pick up a sandwich for me."

"Okay, Mama," was J.R.'s terse reply as he sat down next to his wife with a look of scowling despair on his face. When Sue Ellen reached out to pat his knee reassuringly, he pulled his leg away.

Harlan Danvers was a trusted man in all of Dallas. As the Ewing family physician, he had been the main medical advisor to the family, even helping to deliver their youngest son. Now, the news he had to give Ellie was not pleasant.

"Ellie," he said quietly when the two had found an isolated corner in the solarium, "I'm not going to hold anything back from you. It's bad. We just finished the cardiac cath test and we found a blockage in several of Jock's arteries. He's lost over eighty percent of the blood flow in three of his arteries, to be exact. At this rate, the mildest heart attack could kill him, and it's just a miracle, frankly, that he isn't dead yet. He's had a severe thrombosis—very severe—and there's probably a lot of damage to the heart.

Ellie was trying her best to be calm and controlled. A moment of crisis is not a moment for hysteria, she thought as she leaned gently on Harlan Danvers' arm and asked, "Is it hopeless then, Harlan?" A surge of panic flooded her body, and her eyes welled up with stinging tears, but she fought her feelings back.

His answer was swift. "Ellie, we have one option in a case like this: open heart surgery. I've called San Antonio for Dr. Robert Bycroft—he's the finest cardiac specialist in the state, and we were lucky to get him. He's on his way to Dallas now. He can try a by-pass graft on Jock and it might just work, if his heart isn't too badly scarred."

"Oh, Harlan. Slow down. I'm having a hard time comprehending everything you're saying. What do you mean by by-pass? Will it save Jock's life?"

"It's like building a detour around the heart, Ellie. We take open arteries from the patient's legs and connect them to his heart. It's a fairly common procedure these days, and Jock has a good chance for survival if we act fast."

"How fast, Harlan?" Ellie asked, her frightened brown eyes looking up at him pleadingly.

"Right away. If I have your permission, I'd like to begin prepping Jock and have him in surgery in an hour."

What could she say? Ellie hardly knew what to think. Her husband was dying, that much was clear, and the operation might be able to save his life.

"What do I have to sign, Harlan."

In over forty years of practice, Harlan had few patients he viewed with such affection. Ellie Ewing was a true lady—mature, understanding and warm. In an uncharacteristic gesture, he leaned over and kissed her on the cheek. "I'll have somebody bring the papers to you. Meanwhile, why don't you duck in and say hello to your old man? He was asking for you." And with that the doctor hurried off to begin preparations for the six-hour surgical procedure that might save Jock's life.

Ellie took a deep breath before she pushed through the door she had been watching with such longing all afternoon. Turning an antiseptic corner, she saw Jock's room and entered it.

Jock was ashen. He lay motionless, a tube protruding from his right wrist. When she saw him, Ellie had to make a conscious effort to hide her shock.

"Ellie—" His voice was a pale imitation of itself, a grave whisper that should have been a clear boom.

He knew in an instant that he must look very bad. Ellie couldn't hide her feelings no matter how she tried.

"Jock," she answered, doing her best to duplicate her usual no-nonsense tone. "How are you feeling, dear?"

Her husband groaned in response.

"They want to open me up, Ellie. Did they tell you?"

"Yes. I just talked with Harlan. You're going to have a triple by-pass and then you're going to be fine."

"Did Harlan say all that?"

"He said you needed the operation."

Through his pain, Jock smiled ironically. "Well, Ellie—you sure were right about that bacon."

At first she wasn't sure whether or not Jock was joking with her, but then, the impish look on his face gave him away.

"I want you to put that right on my grave for the whole world to see: 'Ellie was right.'"

Despite herself, Ellie laughed gently. "Listen you. I was right and don't you forget it, but it's not going on any gravestone because there isn't going to be any gravestone for a long, long time!"

Saying it almost convinced her.

"Harlan said they're getting you the best cardiac surgeon in the state."

"Well, I should hope so, considering what the bill for all this is going to be," was the reply. "How are the boys? They're here with you, aren't they?"

Ellie hesitated. She felt Bobby's absence keenly and knew that it would hurt Jock to the quick. "J.R. is outside. He's been pacing up and down the corridor for over two hours. But Bobby—well, he's on his way. Pam was finally able to reach him in Houston and she said he'd be back as soon as he could."

Jock sighed and settled his head back in the pillow, a pained expression on his face. "I don't know Ellie, sometimes I think I failed as a father."

Ellie's denial was genuine as she countered. "Jock! What in heaven's name is making you think that? You were a wonderful father!"

"J.R. and Bobby can't get along. And then there's Gary. I wasn't a father to him at all. Not to

Gary."

The terrible truth settled over the room. What words of comfort could she offer him, she wondered. He and J.R. had shaken Gary's self-confidence down and then cruelly driven him off Southfork. At the time it had broken Ellie's heart, and for years she harbored a secret and not so secret resentment of her husband for his actions. But in recent years, she often wondered if Gary wasn't better off away from Jock and J.R. and the business of Ewing Oil. Maybe in California he could make a new life for himself—one of his own creation. Nevertheless, Jock's admission now was startling. For years he had defended his action against Gary. It was somehow comforting that he knew the truth deep down. Still she had to find a way to comfort him. This was not the time for self-reproach.

"Whatever little problems they have, J.R. and Bobby are wonderful sons. And as for Gary—well, maybe you did make some mistakes—but every parent does! Gary is building his own life now. Besides, what happened between you and him is all in the past now. It's over and done with."

Jock looked up at Ellie with trusting eyes. "Do you forgive me then, Ellie—for Gary? He was always really more your boy than mine."

"Of course I forgive you. And I'm sure he'll do just fine on his own. It was probably the best thing for him."

"If anything happens to me Ellie, keep the family together."

His voice was so sincere, his feelings so vulnerable, that Ellie had to stifle her tears when she answered. "Now, nothing is going to happen, except that you are going to come home a healthy man!"

"Promise me, Ellie. It means everything to me."

"I promise, Jock."

The silence that descended on them took on a calm and healing power. Ellie reached out and gently took her husband's hand, squeezing it slightly.

He was the first to speak. Chuckling softly through his pain, he looked up at his wife.

"Your father didn't give us six months, Ellie."

She laughed, too. "Well, he was certainly wrong. Headstrong as we both are, we raised a fine family and we're still here to tell about it!"

Jock caressed her face with his eyes as he said sincerely and unsentimentally, "You made my life, Ellie." And with that, a nurse appeared to gently escort Ellie from the room.

Outside, time crawled. Dr. Bycroft, the cardiac specialist who had flown in from San Antonio, had time only to hurriedly shake hands with Ellie in the corridor before he sped away to prepare for surgery. Harlan trusted the doctor completely, but Ellie couldn't help thinking the man looked as if he needed a vacation.

Pam arrived breathlessly at the hospital after Sue Ellen and J.R. left, only to find Jock had already been wheeled into surgery. Ellie, who was normally so warm and accepting of her newest daughter-in-law, had little more than a nod for the young woman as she sat staring straight ahead, a dazed look on her face. The long wait had begun.

The taxi sped down San Antonio Avenue as the man in the back seat held his head in his hands. Since he had gotten the call from J.R. hours before, Bobby had been making his way home. The helicopter ride felt interminable and now the taxi, though it was racing, seemed to be taking an unholy amount of time to reach its destination. J.R. had been brutally frank with Bobby on the phone, sparing him no details and laying the situation out in a cool and collected way. Right after Bobby had left in the morning, Jock had collapsed. J.R. had found him, hardly breathing, a man crushed by pain. He had been rushed to Dallas Memorial where nobody knew if he would live or die, and everybody was asking where the hell Bobby was.

Helpless in the back seat, Bobby played back again and again, the conversation he had had with his father earlier in the day like a record on automatic replay. The questions came to him relentlessly. Had their conversation in the morning been the last they'd ever have? Why hadn't he found a way to express his love somehow in the middle of all the upset and confusion.

His daddy had always been so supportive and confident of his abilities. Why hadn't Bobby shown more appreciation? But the worst question—the most unwanted but the most frequent—was whether he had somehow been the cause of his father's heart attack. He remembered with anguish the look in the old man's eyes when he brought up his construction idea and said he couldn't work with J.R. anymore. His daddy's eyes had gone wild for a minute, revealing a deep inner disturbance. Why hadn't Bobby seen that at the time? Why hadn't he reassured his father that something could be worked out with J.R., somehow, if it meant so much to him.

Unaware that the taxi had arrived at the hospital

until the driver turned around and called to him, Bobby paid the fare and raced up the steps of Dallas Memorial. Outside the Intensive Care Unit, he saw his wife and his mother. From the solemn expressions on their faces, Bobby thought for one horrible moment that Jock had died. But when Ellie stood and put her arms out, she whispered distractedly, "He's in surgery, Bobby. All we can do now is pray."

Pam took Bobby's side, bussing his cheek and pressing her hand in his.

"How long?" was all Bobby could ask.

"Another three or four hours," was the grim reply.

"They're doing a triple by-pass."

More than anything at that moment, Bobby wanted to be strong. It was important now; he was the man and his mother needed his strength. But despite himself, hot tears stung his eyes. His father was too vital a man, too strong, to die and leave Ellie a widow. "Oh, Mama," Bobby cried, "I'm so sorry."

Ellie seemed to not hear him as she sat back down, the same dazed look on her face. Bobby and Pam took their places at her side, but instead of inviting their presence, Ellie seemed almost cross.

"If you children don't mind, I would rather be alone now," she sighed heavily.

From Bobby's point of view there was reproach in his mother's voice. He expected it. Why wouldn't she blame him, he thought guiltily. It was only human. "Mama, please forgive me," he muttered, listlessly, his head hung low.

Ellie was confused, but she hadn't the energy to sort out what was going on with her son. He was a grown man and he'd have to take care of his own feelings, however irrational they might be. Maybe later she would talk with him and find out what he meant, but not now. Now, she needed to be alone. She wanted the freedom to cry without anyone else seeing her.

"Please, Bobby. I don't want to be with anyone. I sent J.R. and Sue Ellen away, too. Just leave me alone for a few hours. I'll be fine. In fact, you can pick up some things for me from the house later. I've asked Dr. Danvers to order a cot for me so your father won't have to be alone tonight. Here's a list of what I need."

How efficient Miss Ellie was, Pam thought, even under these dreadful circumstances. Gently kissing her mother-in-law on the cheek, Pam took Bobby's hand and whispered, "Come on, honey. We'll come back."

Bobby allowed himself to be led away like a lost puppy. Down the hall he muttered to Pam, "I'll never forgive myself as long as I live."

"What are you talking about, Bobby?" Pam was incredulous. How could Bobby possibly be blaming himself for what had happened to Jock?

"I told him this morning that I wanted to leave Ewing Oil, Pam—and this is what happened. J.R. told me about it. As soon as I left for the helicopter, Daddy collapsed! It's my fault that he's laying on the operating table now having his heart operated on! I upset him! I caused the whole thing!"

Suddenly, it was all too clear to Pamela. Now she understood why J.R. had insisted on calling Bobby in Houston. When he told her *he* wanted to make the call, she had thought he was offering to free

Pamela so that she could help Miss Ellie get ready to go to the hospital. But it was stupid to think J.R. would ever consider others first, she thought. And how evil of J.R. to make Bobby think he had caused his father to have a potentially fatal episode!

"Your father collapsed after arguing with J.R., Bobby!" Pam said intently, holding onto her husband's arm. "The gardener told me they were on the porch shouting at each other when Jock collapsed! He saw the whole thing! Your father may have been upset with you, but he certainly was upset with J.R. as well. But, honey, nobody is responsible for this! People have heart attacks every day and all those people haven't had a fight with their sons! It's not fair to you to blame yourself and it's not fair to your father, either. How do you think he would feel if he knew you were feeling responsible for the ordeal he's going through now?"

Bobby sighed as a wave of relief passed over him. The things Pam was saying made a lot of sense to him. Stopping in the middle of the busy hospital corridor, Bobby leaned down and kissed her.

"I married the finest woman in the world," he said appreciatively.

Holding hands, the couple made their way to the street. But as they began down the steps of the hospital, they spotted Sue Ellen and J.R. approaching. Watching them from afar Pam thought J.R. looked weary, almost defeated,—it was a look she had never seen on him before.

"J.R.," Bobby said in cautious greeting, stopping as he passed his brother.

"Well, if it isn't my baby brother," was J.R.'s hostile retort. "Nice of you to show up. Too bad you were too late to see Daddy—but then, you always were a Johnny-come-lately, weren't you, Bobby?"

"Look, J.R., this isn't the time for us to be at each other's throats. Our father is in there having very major surgery and we should just be concentrating on his getting better. He may be dying and he needs our support."

"Dying! That's right, Bobby! You damned near killed him with those wild ideas of yours and you know it! What do you think brought that heart attack on, little brother? He was fine this morning, before you came around making trouble! Daddy put his whole life into Ewing Oil. It's bound to kill him when you tell him you don't care about the company and want to run off half-cocked on your own!"

"It wasn't like that, J.R.!" Bobby said trying desperately to control the growing rage inside him.

"And now that you finally decided to show up here at the hospital and join this family, I see you're leaving already," J.R. snapped at his brother. "That was quick. But typical, too, I suppose. It's just like you to desert the family."

Pamela stood in silent fury as her brother-in-law waged his irrational and vicious attack on her husband. She could feel the pressure building in Bobby and gently placed her hand on his arm in supportive restraint. Sue Ellen stepped in front of J.R. as if to constrain him.

"Now, J.R.—Bobby—please, don't fight. I'm sure your daddy would forgive Bobby under the circumstances," she said, somehow making everything worse in her attempt to make it better.

"It's *you* Daddy had the fight with, J.R., not me!"

Bobby said, as reasonably as he could.

"Oh? Is that so?" J.R. taunted Bobby and stepped around his wife to position himself in front of his brother. "Would you like to come a little closer and say that to me?"

"Don't tempt me, J.R.," was Bobby's cool response, though in his eyes a furnace of fury could be seen blazing. If there was one thing J.R. needed, Bobby thought, it was a good solid punch in the face, but he would be damned if he would sink so low as to fight with his brother in front of the hospital while their father was undergoing critical surgery.

J.R. kept it up. Frustrated by Bobby's refusal to strike, he hissed, "Well, why don't I just beat you to the punch, little brother!"

Suddenly, J.R. was lunging at Bobby, aiming for his face with a hard smooth fist. But Bobby dodged artfully, and J.R.'s punch landed full force into the brick building leaving his knuckles a mass of bleeding flesh.

Pamela seized the moment. J.R. was too stunned by the pain in his hand to try again. She tugged at her husband, whispering, "Let's get away from this animal, Bobby. You don't need this."

Pedestrians stopped to gawk as Bobby and Pamela walked briskly away from a distraught Sue Ellen and a fuming J.R. who held his right hand crumpled in his left. "I'll get you another time, little brother!" he screamed like a spoiled child. "You just wait!"

Bobby shuddered as he heard those words but kept walking as fast as he could.

The electric cardiogram monitor beeped peacefully,

its design a series of green, undulating waves that assured Dr. Bycroft that his patient had been kept alive during the grueling open heart surgery when heart and body had been severed from one another. Now, with the last of the stitches in place, he and his operating team finished up their work.

Nodding wearily to his assistants, the cardiac specialist stepped away from the operating table and murmured through the thin gauze pad he wore around his face, "Let's take him off the machine and see how he does, folks." Until now, Jock's heart and lungs had been operated mechanically by the large machine at his side. Now, the new arteries were in place and Jock's heart, which had not been nearly as scarred as they had expected, would face the test of beating on its own.

Quick to follow orders, one of the nurses stepped to the machine and placed her fingers on its blue lever. The air of expectancy in the room was keen, as the life of the man on the table before them hung in the balance. Many of the members of the operating team had never experienced an open heart surgery before this one and they knew that no matter how smoothly the procedure seemed to go, the operation could be considered successful only when the patient breathed on his own.

When the blue lever was depressed, they waited. It was only a fraction of a second, but it felt like an eternity to Robert Bycroft. He had performed enough by-pass surgery to know that something was wrong. Then, confirming his worst feelings, the monitor behind the team, watched diligently by one of the assistants, began registering an eerie hum as the leaping green line went flat. Jock Ewing was, technically speaking, a dead man.

Wasting not an instant, Bycroft was in place, a defibrillator, used to shock a heart into beating, in hand. Touching the paddles to Jock's chest, he sent a surge of electrical energy through the dead man's body. The line remained flat.

"Again," the surgeon said firmly, with only a slight chill in his voice. Another powerful surge jumped through the paddles on the dead man's chest.

Every person in the operating room stood at attention, their breaths sharply inhaled, except for the man monitering the EKG machine. He panted lightly as drops of sweat formed on his brow. The flat line began taking shape. Slowly, it formed the peaks and valleys of a normal heart beat, and a sense of relief filled the operating room.

Bycroft chuckled softly. The man who lay asleep in front of him would live after all. Not only that, the renewed blood flow through his arteries would give him a vigor he probably hadn't known in years. It was moments like this that made his profession worth all the stress and long hours. Leaning over the operating table, he whispered softly into his patient's unhearing ear: "My friend, live and be well—you have truly been born again." Then, tugging at his surgical gloves, he nodded to the orderlies who were waiting by the door to wheel Jock to the recovery room.

Chapter Five

The family had been waiting two weeks for Jock's return and finally the big day had arrived. During Jock's absence, Bobby had stopped going into the office and had taken Jock's place as the family rancher. He was given the honor of chauffeuring his father home from the hospital.

Ellie had had the servants busy polishing the silver and cleaning Southfork from top to bottom all morning and the day before as well. Jock's homecoming was coincidentally on the same day as their fortieth wedding anniversary, and although she was sure it would have slipped Jock's mind, as it always did, she wanted the day to be as celebratory as possible. She had made sure everyone in the family planned to be home for supper—J.R., Sue Ellen, Bobby, Pam, and Lucy. Lucy was at an age when she seldom spent what was known as "quality time" with her family. She was either out with friends or on the phone, and Ellie had treated it as a major coup when the girl agreed without argument to attend Jock's homecoming dinner.

Ellie sighed thinking about her granddaughter. She had more than a touch of Gary's recklessness in her, and she seemed to be drifting away from the family as he did as a boy. No matter how hard she and Jock had tried to raise her to be a conventional Texas woman, their efforts were in vain. Lucy was the cause of a lot of stress around Southfork, with her unknown boyfriends and poor grades in school. Jock never came right out and said it, but Ellie knew that he was deeply disappointed in his only grandchild.

Putting that unpleasant thought from her mind by telling herself Lucy's teenage rebellion was typical and only of a garden variety nature, Ellie began surveying the mansion on her way to the kitchen. The servants had done their work well. The wooden bannisters on the main stairway had a renewed, rich luster. The sun sparkled from the dining room chandelier sending tiny rainbows over the room. And the brass trimmings of the fireplace gleamed. Southfork had never looked better, she thought, not even when Gramma Southworth used to scrub it on her hands and knees because she thought no one cared for it as well as she.

In the kitchen Ellie stopped to talk to Teresa who was already beginning dinner preparations and going over the menu for tomorrow's breakfast. There would be no bacon, and no croissants. Instead the table would be laden with yogurt, fresh fruit juices, strawberries and dark brown bread. Ellie wanted to make sure Teresa had been well-informed about the new style of cooking she wanted for all meals at Southfork. This new diet was no longer just a preference but an absolute must. By-pass operations offered new hope, but a fatty diet would clog the arteries again in a few years unless the patient took on a new style of living and eating. Ellie had searched hard for recipes that were sure to please Jock without offending his restricted diet. She hoped he wouldn't even notice the new cuisine, as she intended to call it. Yesterday, Ellie had made sure Teresa had studied the new recipes and was ready to put them into effect. Tonight's menu was broiled fish, baked potato sans butter or sour cream, and fresh broccoli. Dessert would be fresh nectarines and peaches served with decaffeinated tea. Ellie was satisfied.

The horn of Bobby's red Mercedes tooted playfully. Ellie ran to the huge white door, stopping for only a second to apply a fresh coat of muted pink lipstick and pat her hair into place. Then she threw open the door and ran across the lawn. Jock was a little thinner than he had been when she had last seen him at home, but he was still her beloved Jock—alive and well. Running to him like a young girl, Ellie threw her arms gently around his neck— mindful of the twelve-inch incision in his chest—and warmly kissed him on the lips.

"Darling—you look wonderful!" Ellie said happily, tears of sheer gratitude filling her eyes.

Jock smiled proudly—almost like a young boy. Then he turned to Bobby with a wink. "If I'd have known a by-pass would get me that response, I might have tried it a lot sooner!"

"Oh, you!" was his wife's response as she put her arm around his waist and walked slowly and carefully with him to the entrance of the mansion.

Inside, Jock made his way up the stairs on Bobby's arm as Ellie went off to have Teresa make some hot decaffeinated tea for her husband, and Raoul carried the bags into the master bedroom. The minute Raoul left, Jock called to Bobby and pressed a hundred dollar bill in his hand.

"Go get your mother some flowers and a bottle of some perfume, will you Bobby?" he asked fondly. "And pick out a nice card that I can sign. Today's our anniversary, you know, and I don't want her to think I forgot."

Bobby stood in front of his father in happy amazement. Jock's forgetfulness of his anniversaries was a kind of tradition that was well-documented in the Ewing family history! Jock was famous for remembering the date of the event two weeks, three weeks, even months after the appointed date. Fortunately, Miss Ellie was an understanding and unsentimental woman and she had easily forgiven her husband's forgetfulness over the years, enjoying it as a joke instead of taking it as an affront.

Now, looking at his father, Bobby was struck by how ardent Jock was. "But Daddy, you were in the hospital. I'm sure Mama would understand if you didn't get her anything this year."

"Why should she have to understand, Bobby? She deserves a hell of a lot more than I'd ever be able to give her anyway! She stuck by me all these years and I want her to be damned sure I appreciate it and care! You just get the best stuff they have in Dallas—but nothing too sweet, okay? I hate that sweet stuff. Makes me think I'm going to a funeral instead of sitting next to a woman. And don't scrimp on the flowers. A nice spray of orchards might be nice and those freesia she likes so much. White ones. Enough to fill the place. Here," he said, reaching in his pants pocket for his wallet, "better take this too." Jock pressed another three hundred crisp dollar bills in his son's hand.

"Well, I guess I'll lie down for a while, son. The doctor said it would be six weeks before I was fully recuperated, and I'm feeling a little tired from the ride home. Besides, your mother will like it if she walks in and finds me resting in bed like a good boy. I don't want to worry her any more than I already have." Jock dutifully sat on the edge of his bed, swung his legs around and lay down with a resigned look on his face.

Bobby smiled on the way down the stairs. He was lucky to have parents who loved each other so deeply. Maybe, he thought, that was why he was so happy with his own wife. Like his mother, Pam was a very fine person—a woman who had her feet on the ground, and had a great sensitivity and understanding of others. The fact that she was incredibly beautiful and a thrilling lover were almost parenthetical to the happiness he felt with her. She was his best friend and supporter and his dearest sweetheart and mistress all rolled into one fabulous wife.

Just last night they had talked about possibly having a child. Bobby was ready for fatherhood—he felt it in his bones. As for Pam, she had said she might be ready, too, though she had originally wanted to wait a few years to start a family. When they were first married, she had accidently become pregnant and had suffered a disastrous miscarriage. The incident seemed to hurt her very deeply, and they hadn't spoken of a child for months afterwards. But now, maybe Pam had healed, Bobby thought. Last night, she confessed she needed a change. Being a member of the "idle rich" was new for her—she was unused to having so much free time and so little work.

Talking together as they lay in bed after making love, they had decided that Pam should have a complete gynecological checkup before they stopped using any birth control. If the doctor gave them the go-ahead, they would talk more. Pam told him honestly that she was leaning toward becoming a mother soon, but that she wasn't entirely sure about it. He thought she sounded eager, but she was a little afraid. In his heart, he believed she was ready. Now, Bobby thought, getting back into his car, if he could only get his work life straight, his life would be perfect.

Since Jock had had the heart attack, Bobby had not returned to the offices in downtown Dallas. His construction idea was still alive—Rory was making a proposal that would take a few weeks—and so, to fill in the time, Bobby was working with Ray on the ranch.

What a relief it had been to get out of the office and away from all the tension that he had been experiencing at Ewing Oil. The tight feeling in his chest that he got whenever he walked into J.R.'s office had left him completely, and Bobby felt like a new man. Being out with Ray in the open air and working with the earth had been just the tonic Bobby needed. No wonder his daddy loved it so.

Bobby's only leftover fear was that J.R. would do something terrible—he didn't know what—to "get back" at Bobby for leaving Ewing Oil. After their run-in at the hospital, the brothers had barely spoken to one another. But to everyone's surprise, J.R. had taken Bobby's absence very well. He seemed almost happy about it. Having a brother at the office must have been hard on J.R., too, Bobby thought kindly. Now that he was gone, it was a blessing all the way around.

Even Jock had seemed to accept Bobby's decision to leave. It had been hard to face his father in the hospital with the news that he planned to help Ray Krebbs on the ranch for a while until he sorted things out for himself. Jock had just been through an incredible ordeal of his own, after all. But Bobby wanted his father to know from him, not from anybody else, about the time he was taking off from Ewing Oil. Working on the ranch seemed like a natural way to be productive while taking a break from the office. Bobby hadn't had the heart to tell his father that the construction idea was still very much on his mind—not after the way his father had first reacted—but that too would come in time. Maybe he would come to accept that eventually. But right now the main thing Jock had to concentrate on was his health. After he regained that, Bobby promised himself, he'd get J.R. and the three men could work something out. Maybe Ewing Construction could be a direct branch of Ewing Oil rather than a separate company.

Sue Ellen stood in the middle of Neiman-Marcus twisting her handkerchief into a tight ball in the palm of her hand. She was in the middle of a full-blown panic attack. J.R. had been very direct with his instructions. She was to buy Jock and Miss Ellie an anniversary gift that would make any other anniversary gift they received look sick. But what? He hadn't offered any suggestions—just the threat that it had better be something wonderful.

Sue Ellen had sat for hours in her room, thin gold pen in hand, trying to write out some of her ideas. None had come. At last, when she looked at her wristwatch and saw the time creeping towards 3:30, she had had Raoul bring her car around so that she could race to Dallas and pick up something.

What could you buy for people like Jock and Ellie, she thought. All *he* really liked were oil and guns and hunting and cows and such, and all *she* really liked were her flower gardens. Yet, if she appeared at dinner with wrapped boxes of bullets and tulip bulbs, she smirked, J.R. would surely be angry. The truth was her in-laws had more money than they could ever spend so there was no such thing as a practical gift. The gift would have to be extravagant—but what?

"May I help you?" the clerk asked, intruding on Sue Ellen's internal chaos like a nurse waking a patient to take a pill. Sue Ellen's eyelids fluttered. Somehow, she found herself in the notions department staring at accoutrements for closets and bathrooms. Her eyes fell on a strange instrument resembling an old-fashioned pants presser, but made of fine china. It was an electric towel heater, the clerk explained jocularly. You hung the towels on it like a regular towel rack, but they heated up and were toasty warm when your bath was finished. Sue Ellen was pretty sure her in-laws had no such thing. And who wouldn't like the idea of wrapping up in a heated towel after the bath? It was perfect.

"Well, I think I'll take it," Sue Ellen said without much argument as she pointed to the odd-shaped, free-standing rack. "How much is it, please?"

The clerk was confident. "Oh, that piece is imported from England. It's fully guaranteed for five years and uses very little electricity."

Sue Ellen felt her heart racing. Would the woman never stop describing the damned thing and get to the point? "Yes?" she said, feigning interest.

"And it happens to be on sale for only $325. Shall I wrap it or would you like to have it delivered?"

Sue Ellen shook her head vigorously. The gift was far too inexpensive. "No, thank you. I . . . I don't think it's quite appropriate. My father-in-law doesn't really use towels."

She was acting stupid and saying stupid things and she knew it. Her face was burning red and she could feel herself sweating enough to fill the Rio Grande River. She had to get out of there, move on to another department—but she had to find *something* and bring it home tonight!

Wandering past the cosmetics, Sue Ellen comforted herself with a $50 purchase of a special European night cream. There was no getting around it. She was getting older. The little lines spreading out from the corners of her eyes told the same sad story for all "former" beauty queens. Somehow, she had always thought she would be immune to the effects of time. She had only been in her early twenties when she was crowned Miss Texas—and a year and a half later, she had married the handsome, young, successful J.R. Ewing. Everything was so rosy then. But now, lines were appearing around her eyes and she was becoming an ordinary Texas matron—one with no children.

"Stop it," Sue Ellen muttered to herself firmly as she slipped her small purchase into her handbag. Once, when she was single and very depressed, she had consulted a psychologist who had told her it was dangerous to think of oneself as powerless. Maybe she was getting older, but that didn't mean she couldn't be happy. She could still have a child and she could still make her marriage work somehow. She had to have confidence, that was all. She had to act on her own behalf, take charge of her own life.

Wandering into the art department, Sue Ellen mastered the painful thoughts of panic and self-doubt and was determined to make a purchase that would be spectacular! In her heart she thought that her taste was really superior to that of the other Ewing women. She had that thought ever since Miss Ellie ordered red velvet curtains for the main living room. So buying Jock and Miss Ellie a present was merely an opportunity to display that taste.

"May I help you?" This time the voice was male. A small dark man with a moustache was presenting himself at her service. His voice was gentle and oddly comforting.

"Yes. I need to buy something for my in-laws' fortieth wedding anniversary. And I really would like something very special. They have a large house and I thought they might appreciate some original art work."

She was starting to sound stupid to herself again, and she vowed to stay as quiet as possible from now on.

"Well, well . . ." said the clerk in a conspiratorial

tone, as if he and Sue Ellen were old and dear friends, "how utterly perfect." He began to laugh as if he were thinking of the most delightful joke he'd ever heard. "I have the most splendid gift. We got it in from Italy just yesterday. We weren't going to put it on the floor because the Governor's wife is so interested in this artist, but she informed us that she was leaving the country for a few weeks. I suppose no one would be any the wiser if I sold it to you."

With that the clerk disappeared and Sue Ellen began looking at the various *objets d'art* around her. At first her confidence held strong. But as the minutes passed and she looked at everything in the department, she was struck with the thought that she didn't really know the first thing about art. Her so-called great taste was nothing more than her own inflated opinion of herself. The same painful haunting thoughts came back to her. Her age . . . her lines . . . her childlessness . . .

"Impressive, isn't it?" The clerk's voice broke through he litany of problems in a comforting way. Sue Ellen looked up, grateful to be called back to Dallas from her lonely nightmare.

Before her stood a large black "thing." Was it onyx? No. But it was carefully mounted on a bronze stand that had the artist's signature burned in it.

"This piece is the work of Italy's newest, foremost sculptor, Mario Osborno. You can tell from the sleek lines that the piece is neo-classic, but it's set in an abstract mode to achieve the look of metal in its natural state."

Sue Ellen considered the piece, her left heel beginning to blister in the black pumps she was wearing. She must have walked six miles of Dallas department stores. And now she was here with this sweet man with the moustache. "Metal in its natural state." Wasn't that something like Jock's life work? Hadn't he made his fortune by finding oil in its natural state?

"How much is the piece please?" Sue Ellen asked shyly.

The clerk coughed with embarrassment. "It's, um, well, madame—Osborno has quite a reputation. The piece is six thousand dollars."

Sue Ellen smiled and breathed deeply with relief. "It's perfect. Have a man put it in my car, please. I'll take it."

There was no better time for Ellie than the times her family was gathered together around the dining room table. Watching them that night, she was filled with a deep sense of gratitude. How handsome her two sons were and how beautiful their wives. Even Lucy had made an effort to fit in with the family by appearing in a lovely pink dress instead of her usual sweat shirt.

But the crowning presence of the evening was Jock. What better anniversary present could she possibly have then to have him home with her again, recuperating but beyond a doubt on the road to health.

Bowing her head as J.R. said a simple grace, Ellie was moved to tears—tears of appreciation and love. Jock was home. He was well. Smiling at him across the table she vowed to make the next years of their lives the best years. God had given her a precious gift and she was going to treasure it.

If the dinner was not to his taste, Jock said

nothing. Instead he complimented his wife on the fine menu and ate uncomplainingly that which he would have mercilessly mocked just a few weeks ago. It was clear to both husband and wife that his experience at Dallas Memorial Hospital had left Jock a changed man. He was calmer, more comfortable. He had stopped smoking—this time for real—joking with Ellie that his motivation was simple: whenever he wanted a smoke, he closed his eyes and remembered what it felt like to be brought into the Intensive Care Unit. After an experience like that, he claimed, he would have no trouble stopping.

Throughout dinner, Pam noticed Jock and Ellie's eyes meeting from time to time. It was as if there were a magnetic charge running between them. Bobby noticed it, too, and he also basked in its glow.

After supper, the group gathered 'round the living room to present Jock and Ellie with their anniversary gifts.

Lucy had bought Jock a radio with earphones so that he could listen to music or the news on the four mile walks he had been ordered to take daily. Ellie presented her husband with tickets for a trip to Hawaii. After he recuperated, they would fly to San Francisco and see a friend for a few days before embarking on a trip to the magical isles. They needed a vacation after all this, she had reasoned.

"Somehow, through the busy years, we never found the time to travel together. That is all going to change now," Ellie said, as Jock appreciatively bussed her on the cheek and put the tickets in the pocket of the maroon robe he was wearing.

Jock leaned over to Bobby and whispered in his

ear: "What did you do with my package, son?"

Ellie looked confused as Bobby jumped up and signaled to Teresa. A moment later, three Southfork servants entered, their faces nearly hidden by the huge bouquets of flowers they carried. Setting her flowers at Miss Ellie's feet, Teresa then handed Jock a small, silver-wrapped box.

"For you, Ellie," Jock said softly. "I'm just sorry it isn't more."

Ellie opened the box carefully, tears streaming down her face. "You remembered, Jock," she murmured, and gently lifted a pearl and ruby ring from the black velvet. "How beautiful," she cried.

Jock looked at Bobby in wonder, but Bobby just winked. "All the perfume stores were closed," he joked.

The next package was terribly large. The family wondered aloud what it could possibly be as they watched Raoul carry it in from the kitchen. The normally strong and uncomplaining Raoul was wincing with pain as he set the package at Jock's feet.

Everyone smiled falsely as the scuplture was unwrapped. Looking at it out of the package, no one knew what to say. The uncomfortable silence was broken only when Jock asked sincerely, "What the hell *is* that?"

"It's a sculpture," Sue Ellen replied weakly. "I thought it would look nice in your den."

Jock was as gracious as he could be. He looked at the piece with insincere admiration as Ellie tactfully told Sue Ellen the piece was lovely. Pam and Bobby politely agreed. But J.R. glared at his wife when no one else was looking at her. Sue Ellen flushed deeply and poured herself another glass of wine.

The last present was from Bobby and Pam. It was a leather bound photograph album with the name EWING embossed in gold on the front. Inside, Bobby and Pam had made copies of favorite family photos through the years. Jock and Ellie laughed at the old-fashioned sepia pictures of themselves as children. There were photos of Jock and Ellie as newlyweds stepping into a 1935 black Ford complete with a running board. Next came pictures of the boys: J.R. in his satin baby bunting, he and Bobby tussling in the sandbox, Gary seated on a horse. Then there was a photo of Lucy, one month old, lying naked on a fur blanket. Lucy shrieked with embarrassment as the others oohed and aahed about how cute she was. There were wedding pictures—Sue Ellen and J.R. with their half-dozen attendants, Bobby and Pam in a simple snapshot outside the Justice of the Peace. But Jock seemed captivated by the photos of the babies. Again and again he turned back to them—J.R., Bobby, Gary, Lucy. They had grown up before he knew it, and he missed the little people in the pictures. The house had seemed so much more alive when there were little children running about trying his patience and winning his heart.

"Hell, if you folks really want to make me happy, why don't you get busy making me some heirs! It's been too long a time since we had a baby around here and I miss it!"

There was a moment of silence after his frank remark. Sue Ellen broke the quiet by saying, "J.R. and I plan to start a family real soon, Jock."

Jock leaned back in his chair and chuckled. "I've

heard that same old song for seven years, Sue Ellen. I've about given up on you!"

Sue Ellen smiled widely to cover her pain and poured herself another glass of wine. He hadn't meant to hurt her, but she felt a flush of humiliation nevertheless.

Bobby then spoke up showing an eagerness to please his daddy as strong as J.R.'s. "Well, Daddy. I agree! This family does need some babies! And you may have your wish real soon. Pam has decided to go to a doctor to get a full checkup and then we're going to start trying right away."

"Lord, you people in the younger generation will talk about anything!" Ellie said, shaking her head in amusement as well as embarrassment.

"Well, maybe we'll wait a *little* while, Bobby," added Pam looking at her husband with a shocked expression on her face. "I don't know if I'm really ready for a baby yet."

"Oh, hell! You're ready!" Jock said, happily. "In my day, you were ready the day you said 'I do.' We didn't have to go thinking about this and thinking about that before we took care of business!"

Ellie wanted to smoothe her husband's roughness.

"Believe me, Pam. No woman is ever completely ready for a baby! No matter how much you prepare it always takes you by surprise—the sheer work of it—and the tremendous joy. But of course, the timing is up to you," added Ellie with a smile. Pam hugged her mother-in-law warmly as Sue Ellen turned away.

Was it really after eleven o'clock already? The homecoming dinner had been wonderful, but it was time to tuck Jock in. The family members said their goodnights on the mansion stairway and made their way to their second floor bedrooms.

How wonderful, Ellie thought, closing the door to their master suite. She had her husband at home, hale and hearty, and soon she might have a grandchild to tend to as well. My cup runneth over, Ellie thought to herself as she lay down next to the man she had loved for so long, for her first truly peaceful night's sleep in weeks.

Chapter Six

Bobby watched his wife undress. Although they had just kissed Ellie and Jock goodnight in the festive, light spirit of the evening, secretly he was upset. What had Pam meant when she looked his father straight in the eye and said that she might want to wait a while before they had a baby? Looking at her now, he marveled at how anger and love could coexist so closely. He was flooded with a warm feeling for her, yet she had disappointed him tonight and left him feeling confused and in the dark about an issue that was so important to them both.

Pam was subdued as she lifted one slender leg after the other to remove her stockings. The evening had been marred for her, too, when Bobby openly volunteered in front of his parents and in front of the entire family, that she and Bobby were planning to start a family of their own right away. That really hadn't been fair of him, she thought. After all they had just begun discussing a baby in private. Now she felt a certain pressure about the whole thing that she didn't want to feel. The light that had shone in Ellie and Jock's eyes at the mere mention of a grandchild was a big pressure in itself, and Pam didn't like it one bit.

Bobby cleared his throat. He had decided to be direct. In the time since he had fallen in love with Pam, he had learned the value of open and direct communication. When they were first dating, he had tried to hide from her any uncomfortable feelings he had, but Pam's patient and tolerant love had convinced him that true intimacy required nothing less than the complete truth. And this was a moment when he needed an answer from her. She was brushing her hair at the vanity, the lamp beside her casting a warm glow on the russet strands. How to begin, Bobby thought. He didn't want to ride roughshod over her feelings—he was sensitive to the issue of having a baby after all. And yet, he couldn't help being angry at her for not wanting to plunge ahead as generations of people had done since the beginning of time.

"What was that all about, downstairs?" he began, trying to sound light, but succeeding only in sounding like an old-fashioned husband who feels he owns his wife and all her feelings.

"All what, Bobby?" was Pam's sincere response.

"Well, I thought it was more or less settled, our having a baby." There, he had said it, he thought. Now the ball was in her court.

"Settled? We just started talking about it a couple of days ago, Bobby." Pam had turned in her chair to face him, the mirror behind her reflecting her graceful neck and back. But Bobby wasn't noticing that; he was too busy trying to sound mature. He

79

didn't want to fan the fire of an issue that burned with intensity inside him.

"But, Pam, you told me you wanted children. You told me that when you married me and you told me that last week. When you had the miscarriage you were distraught. You said you wanted to try again right away except for the fact that the doctor told you to wait a few months. And those months have gone by, haven't they? You even have an appointment with Dr. Wagner tomorrow, don't you?" Bobby's eyes were intense.

Pam felt his gaze burning into her like an inquisitor as he punched out every question. She hated this kind of questioning. The answer to every question Bobby asked was "yes"—but that didn't mean she was ready to get pregnant right away.

Pam drew a breath before she answered. She didn't want to fight with Bobby and yet she was angry now, too. This was the time to think first and speak later—to control the angry feelings that were rising in them both.

"Yes, I have an appointment with the doctor and yes, I do want children. But, truly, Bobby—I don't know about it right now! We're still awfully young, and maybe we should just enjoy some time alone together before having babies." Pam looked at her husband with open, questioning eyes. He looked as though he had been hit.

"You know I love you very much, so it isn't from a lack of love that I might want to wait. And it doesn't have anything to do with not wanting children. It's just a matter of timing." She had put down the brush and was looking at him directly, her eyes wide and vulnerable.

Bobby walked to her and gently put his hands on hers. His voice had a pleading quality to it when he spoke. "Come on, Pammy—you saw them down there. My mother and father aren't getting any younger, you know, and . . ."

Pam withdrew her hands from his and put them on his shoulders so that she could look him straight in the eyes. "Bobby, this isn't a decision that anybody else has anything to do with except us. Having a baby isn't about having an heir for your father or a hobby for your mother. It's a child's life we're talking abut and it's too important to be decided because of social pressure."

Bobby's young wife had cut him off in an un-characteristic way. He felt a chill in her words, but he couldn't deny the truth of what she was saying. Nevertheless, he found himself almost shouting at her—shouting things he knew weren't true.

"Is that what it's all about? You resent my parents? You don't want to live at Southfork? Well, I told you when we first got married that we didn't have to live here. If you want, we can buy a house wherever you want!"

"Bobby, calm down. Now this hasn't got anything to do with where we live, honey. And I happen to be very fond of both of your parents, so it isn't that! I'm very happy living here, in fact. It's our home and I know you love it. And it suits me just fine."

"But you said you were getting bored! Didn't you say that not two nights ago—or was I imagining it, Pam? You told me having a baby might be a good thing for you!"

Pam was unruffled. "That's true, Bobby. But

when I gave it a little more thought, I realized that boredom is a poor reason to bring a baby into the world! If I'm bored I should do something about that—like go back to work or something. Then, when I really and truly want a *baby*—not just something to do with my free time, well that's when we should start a family."

Bobby slumped onto the bed. "Women," he muttered.

Pam slipped to the other side. "It's no big deal, really. We will have a child, just not right now. Let me just think about it a little more."

Bobby shrugged as if he didn't care, though the look on his face betrayed his casual behavior. "Okay," he said, with a deadness in his voice.

Pam hesitated. Maybe this was not the ideal time to bring up her news, but she had to do it sometime and since they were clearing the air, why not now?

"Bobby," she began, "I ran into Liz Craig again and she would really like me to come back to The Store. The new buyer is getting married and she's given them notice. Liz told me she'd be thrilled if I'd even consider coming back. She said she could even get me a hundred dollar a week raise."

Bobby look incredulous. "Pam! You're a wealthy woman! What the hell do you want a job for? Most women in your position would be thrilled that they didn't have to get up every morning and slave away for other people all day!"

Pam's eyes narrowed as she looked at her husband with intense concentration. She spoke slowly to him, as if he were a young boy. "I would like to feel productive. You can understand that, can't you? Isn't that what you've always complained about since you went to work with J.R.? I want to feel useful during the day when you're out doing what you have to do. I only want what you want, Bobby!"

Bobby could hardly believe what he was hearing. Why would a person like Pam, who had worked her entire life to earn enough money just for groceries, want to go to a job when she had enough money to burn? It didn't make any sense. Sure, she wanted to feel productive, but why couldn't she feel productive just being his wife? Wasn't he important enough for her?

"Great! You want to work? I'll put you to work! We need somebody to water the horses right here on the ranch. I was going to put an ad in the paper. Short hours and lots of fringe benefits. You get to smell horse dung all day!"

Now it was Pam's turn to look incredulous.

"Bobby Ewing, listen to yourself!"

The two young lovers stopped for a second and regarded each other silently. There was an unspoken message in their eyes. "You are difficult, you know!" they both thought, looking at each other.

In a flash, the pillows began flying as they each picked one up then ducked from the other's blow.

"You!" they giggled as they tried to bop each other into submission.

"Oh, yeah?"

"Yeah!"

"Oh, yeah?"

"Yeah!"

Bobby and Pam tussled, laughing and fighting at the same time. But the merriment had an edge to it as they released their frustrations by pounding each other mercilessly. Finally, when it was clear neither could win, they leaned back on the bed in breathless exhaustion.

"I love you," Bobby said, looking into his wife's eyes. Then he added with a hint of sarcasm, "You're my working-class hero."

"And I love you," she answered, melting into his arms. "You're my ne'er-do-well prince, but please, try to understand."

"I may understand," he said, drawing her even closer, and I may love you very very much—but I don't have to love any of your screwy ideas about going to work and putting off having a baby! And, remember, you won't be able to put it off too long. You did make a promise. Will you still go to the doctor tomorrow?

"Of course. I want to. Just give me a year or two, honey, we have plenty of time. I want to be the best mother I can be and I think I need to grow up a little more. That's all."

Bobby reached out for his wife tenderly, stroking her hair and feeling the warmth of her body close to him. Then, she turned and gently pressed her mouth onto his and they fell back together on the bed. "I love you," she murmured softly in his ear.

His kiss was his response sending an electric thrill through her body. "I love you, too—very much," he said nuzzling her neck.

Their "fight" was over and now the loving would begin. Pam relaxed into his arms.

"Let's make a baby tonight," he whispered into her ear.

She wanted to scream, "Where have you been all

night?" She wanted to scream, "Why don't you listen to me?"

But before she could pull away from him to speak, he whispered, "Just kidding," and they were swept away together.

Unnoticed by anyone, Sue Ellen poured herself a fourth glass of wine as her husband said goodnight to his parents. She then brought it up to their rooms, half hidden by her flowing velvet skirt, and placed it on her vanity behind a huge bottle of French perfume. She and J.R. undressed wordlessly.

Sue Ellen went into the bathroom and selected her most alluring peignoir from the rack behind the door. It was made of sheer black silk with handmade black lace trimming on the part that gently fell over her full and lovely breasts. When she breathed, however lightly, the material parted, revealing her trembling vulnerability.

Slipping into high-heeled, backless, black satin slippers with feather trimming on them, Sue Ellen glanced quickly at the mirror. She was alluring. She knew it and he *had* to know it. It was an outfit that no man could resist. Even the salesgirl had told her that. He could not ignore her tonight. After this evening's disaster, having a baby had become more important than ever!

Sue Ellen had been stung deeply when Jock laughingly told her he had "given up on her" as far as producing a grandchild was concerned. Everyone had "given up" on her, she thought bitterly, but they didn't realize that *she* hadn't given up, and she wasn't so old that she couldn't have a child either. But she needed some cooperation from J.R.

Back in the bedroom her husband sat in bed reading. Sue Ellen wordlessly turned the radio on to an easy listening station and turned the dimmer down slightly so that the lights in the room became soft and sensuous.

"Honey," J.R. said, without looking up, "could you put the light back on? I'm not through with this."

Sue Ellen stood by the wall sensuously shaking her head "no." She walked to her vanity and drank the wine down in one quick gulp. She needed the fortification. Tonight, she would not take no for an answer.

Turning toward J.R., Sue Ellen glided toward the bed losing her balance for a split second but recovering it as she spread her silk negligee on the covers. "Now I have you where I want you," she said daringly, tossing his paper aside, the wine giving her actions a certain boldness.

J.R. smelled the alcohol on her breath. There was nothing uglier to him than a drunken woman, and the thought of kissing her when she was in that condition made him sick to his stomach.

Her hands were reaching for him, violating him with a forceful aggression—aggression he felt was suited to a tart but unbecoming in a wife.

"Sue Ellen, you're drunk."

"I'm not drunk. I'm sexy. And I want you. Now."

She had tried waiting patiently for his attention—tried it for years. Now she was desperate. He *had* to make love with her, otherwise her life was a waste. She would shrivel up—an unloved, childless woman with no one to comfort her in her old age. The more wine she had drunk, the sadder her plight seemed to her. By now, her self-image was pathetic, and only the physical reassurance a husband could give her would do any good.

"Honey, what the hell has gotten into you lately? You've been acting like a tramp." Sometimes nothing but the truth would do, J.R. thought. Maybe it would shock Sue Ellen back into acting normally.

"But that's what you like, isn't it, J.R.? I can give you what those women give you. Try me." Closing her eyes, she leaned back and waited for his heated response.

J.R. found the glasses she had tossed aside with the paper, a slow fury rising up inside him. The thought of his wife drinking and behaving like a fool made him sick. Sue Ellen had certainly become a shoddy imitation of the woman he had married, he thought.

When he had first met Sue Ellen, she was a real lady. She was a beauty queen after all, winner of the Miss Texas competition, sought after by the richest and handsomest men in the state. Before they met, he had seen her at the pageant where he was working as a judge. She attracted him immediately as a young lady with looks and class and he began courting her vigorously, sending yellow roses to her apartment night after night with mysterious notes of love that just hinted J.R.'s at identity. When she finally agreed to have a date with the mysterious Mr. J.R. Ewing, he had taken her to the most expensive places and showered her with attention.

But despite his ardent pursuit, Sue Ellen had refused to let him touch her in any way even remotely sexual. She was kind, but firm, as she told him she was saving herself for the man she would call her husband. J.R. had never had a girl refuse him before. He was rich, young and handsome—a combination that had the most virtuous young ladies of Dallas lifting their skirts in the hopes of becoming Mrs. J.R. Ewing. Sue Ellen was different, and the young Mr. Ewing was smitten.

Her virtue was all the more disarming because her brown eyes seemed to smolder with sensuality. He was ignited with hot desire every time she told him that she "loved her future husband too much" to squander the gift of her virginity on any other man.

J.R. found himself thinking that this "future husband" was getting quite a young lady—virtuous and loyal, but undeniably appealing. Looking at her as she sincerely explained her philosophy of love and marriage, his sexual appetite was whetted until he couldn't take it any more. He began to hint that they would marry in time, thinking he could sample the goods first and decide later, much as one takes a new automobile for a "test run."

But Sue Ellen had refused that request and had seemed so insulted by the suggestion that she threatened to break off with him completely. She began refusing his invitations to dinner and concerts. She had her mother say she wasn't home when he knew she was.

Her refusal to see him became a heady aphrodisiac, heightening his physical interest to the breaking point. He finally broke down and begged her to marry him. The sought-after and attractive Mr. J.R. Ewing had been caught in a web of love and desire.

The night he appeared with a diamond ring in a

little box and actually got down on his knee to propose to her, she let him feel the outline of her soft full breasts under her thin cotton blouse as they embraced chastely. He could hardly contain himself until their wedding night, and had actually convinced her to move up the date. He was afraid for his very manhood if he had to wait for her any longer.

But after their wedding he found out that the sex he had craved so long was not worth the wait. Sue Ellen was inexperienced, clumsy and naive about what pleased a man. And seven years of marriage hadn't changed her in that way. But then, he realized, he had never given her much practice. There was something almost immoral to J.R. about having sex with his wife. The kind of sex he craved—wild, passionate, daring sex—was for ladies of the night, not Daughters of the Alamo.

Sue Ellen, meanwhile, had decided on another tactic. Her voice was muted but the fury in it was barely controlled, like a scream.

"Your brother and that little Barnes girl are going to have a hundred children before we get *one*—and then, who do you think is going to get Southfork when your parents die? And who is going to get to redecorate? Pam! And who will run Ewing Oil? Bobby! And *his* son! That's who! When are you going to wake up! Everything we have is going to slip away if you don't get busy and give me a child!"

J.R. was open-mouthed. How dare this drunken woman talk this way, demanding he perform like a stable stud! He was too angry to speak and thought she would have the good sense to stop when he picked up his paper again as a signal that this discussion was over and done with as far as he was concerned. But Sue Ellen was undaunted.

"Of course, maybe you're incapable. Maybe the great Mr. J.R. Ewing isn't the real man he thinks he is. Maybe your little nighttime visits are to people who know how to deal with impotent men and make them feel good about themselves."

She had gone too far and she knew it.

"J.R., I'm sorry, please." Her voice was a plea. She was begging. "I just want us to love each other."

But, J.R. had walked to the closet where he was selecting a suit of clothes for the next day. He would not be spending his evening at home tonight. He had no intention of listening to her any more.

"Where are you going, J.R.?" she begged.

"Out, darlin'. I need a little night air."

Suddenly, the anger of the past years registered in her voice.

"Oh, no you don't! You're always running off and leaving me! But you can't this time! I won't let you!"

Sue Ellen grabbed hard at his wrist. He shook his hand away. She grabbed it again, harder.

A crash of fire struck across her face.

"Don't ever do that again, darlin'," he said, coolly putting the hand that had struck her in his pocket. "Now, out of my way," he ordered, throwing the door open and hurrying down the stairs.

Sue Ellen hesitated a moment and then flew after him. "You can't do this! You can't leave me again!" Suddenly she didn't care who heard her. Her pain was too great. "I need something for my own! I need someone to hold and something to love," she sobbed.

J.R. was at his car. "I'll see if I can pick up a stray cat at the pound, Sue Ellen," he said before getting in so he wouldn't have to hear more. "A sorry imitation of the woman I married . . ." he muttered to himself, revving up the engine and tearing down Southfork's long driveway.

Laurie's new girl would be a comfort tonight. He would have his way with her—he would prove his superiority until even she begged him to quit.

Sue Ellen stood whimpering in the driveway as she watched her husband's car growing smaller and smaller. Why? she wondered. Why had their marriage gone so wrong? Why was he so vicious and cruel? She had wanted to be a good wife. She had tried so hard. Tears came, the blubbery loose tears of too much drink and too little love.

The lights of J.R.'s car had faded out of view and still she stood there, paralyzed with a deep emotional pain. She couldn't think, couldn't speak.

A light went on suddenly in the house adjacent to the mansion. Ray Krebbs strode out to the driveway, flashlight in hand. Fortunately, no one at Southfork seemed to notice what had happened between her and J.R. The house was dark and quiet.

"Mrs. Ewing, what are you doing out here?" Ray asked. "You'll catch your death."

The Texas night air was cool. Flashing his light near her, Ray realized that J.R.'s wife was almost nude in her sheer gown. But Ray was used to the eccentricities of the very rich. In his years at Southfork he had seen a lot—enough to convince him that the rich are no better and no worse at heart than anyone else. He had known poor men as brutal

as J.R. and as kind as Bobby. But he had always felt a
secret sorrow for Sue Ellen Ewing. To be married to
an animal like J.R. must be a heavy cross to bear—
especially for Mrs. Ewing who seemed like a
sensitive woman, if not a particularly assertive one.

Sue Ellen looked down at her sheer nightgown
and automatically, Ray did too. She pulled her
hands across her breasts in a clumsy effort to hide
them. Out of respect, he tried to hide the impact
that the sight of her firm, full body had on him.

"Come, Mrs. Ewing. I'll walk you to the door."

She had been drinking, he could tell. But her
speech was clear and she seemed coherent.

"No, thank you, Ray," she muttered finally. "I
don't think I want to go back just yet." Tears rolled
down her cheeks.

They stood in the driveway for several seconds
not saying a word. Even he was chilled by the night
air, despite his thick woolen shirt.

After a few moments, Ray gently placed his hand
on her arm and began to lead her to the house. She
was shivering.

"Here we are. Will you be okay, Mrs. Ewing?" he
asked, guiding her gently to the mansion doorway
and turning in retreat.

Suddenly he felt her hand on his arm, imploring
him to stay. She took his hand and looked deeply
into his eyes as she placed it under her negligee.

"Ray, would you be so kind as to show me your
house? I've often admired it but I've never been
inside. I would love to go there now, if you'll let
me."

As she spoke she seemed to be leaning closer and
closer to him. Her touch was irresistible. It took

everything in him to draw away so that he could remove his shirt and place it on her shoulders.

"Ray, I love you. It sounds strange for me to say it, but I've noticed you for years on this ranch. You are a real man, Ray. There aren't many of them left, but you are one."

"Mrs. Ewing," Ray said dumbfounded. She put her arms around his waist and drew him to her. "You don't know what you're saying, Mrs. Ewing. It's late and I think you've had too much to drink."

"*In vino veritas*, Ray. Everything I'm saying is true. I need a man. That's all Ray. I need a man and I'd like it to be you. We don't have to go to your place if you're afraid. You can stay here. Everyone is asleep."

She had pulled him down onto Miss Ellie's rattan sofa. For a split second she seemed calm. "I'm not drunk, Ray. I know what I'm doing," she said clearly.

What could he do? He was used to doing what the Ewings wanted him to do when they wanted him to do it. Now, he was being asked to make love to a Ewing wife—the loneliest woman at Southfork. A woman who had no love in her life. A woman he thought deserved more. In the back of his mind, he'd always dreamed of a moment like this and now it had come. He knelt gently and lifted her up, the scent of her perfume filling his nostrils with a dizzy sensation. The discipline took everything in him, but he had to be sensible, no matter how much she was begging. She deserved better than that.

"Come on, Sue Ellen. We'll go to my place. I'll make you some coffee. We can . . . um . . . be more comfortable there."

Chapter Seven

Ray Krebbs looked at the crumpled cotton sheets on his bed with a sense of wonder as the morning sun poured into his room. Just hours before, Sue Ellen had been with him, murmuring ardent words of love in his ears. She had been so free, so tender, so warm with him—clinging to him with heated desire, and generously giving her womanhood to him.

Then, afterward, they had laughed together as they recalled the first time they'd ever seen one another. Ray had been at the stables working with the horses and Sue Ellen was a bride on J.R.'s arm.

Ray remembered that day intensely, for he thought then that he had never seen a more beautiful woman. And to his utter and complete surprise, Sue Ellen confessed that she had wanted him even then. Many times over the years, she said, she had longed to come to him but she had been too afraid of J.R.'s wrath. Now that was all different. She had finally realized her marriage to J.R. was hopeless and she intended to make a new life for herself somehow.

Running the water for his shave, Ray wondered just how drastically his life would change now. Making love to Mrs. J.R. Ewing had been a daring, even reckless thing to do. J.R. was a ruthless man, and if he ever got wind of last night's events, he would make their lives as miserable as possible and Ray knew it. But how could he have turned her down? Sue Ellen had grown desperate for love during the years of her marriage, and if she had finally decided to get some happiness for herself, who could blame her?

Many times over the years, he had watched the voluptuous brunette as she lay sunning herself by the pool or walking to the house laden with packages from Dallas' most exclusive shops. Sometimes she would smile and wave to him when he brought the order sheets to the house for Jock's okay or when his truck passed her Mercedes at the gate of the ranch. But never in his wildest dreams had he guessed that she noticed him in "that" way.

Well, he supposed, regarding himself in the mirror, that was just typical considering his long-standing problem of low self-esteem. Not having the confidence women liked in a man had cost him more than one relationship. Sometimes he had despaired of ever meeting a female who would return his affection. Night after night he'd sit watching television and longing for a woman of his own—someone he could marry, maybe have kids with. But as the years passed that had seemed more and more like an impossible dream.

But now, everything was different, Ray thought

happily. Now there was Sue Ellen. Just when he was the most lonely, the greatest thing had happened— Sue Ellen Ewing had come to him and told him she loved him—and his head was spinning with happiness. Smiling at his reflection, Ray noticed, as if for the first time, the silver gleam of his hair and the rugged lines on his face. It was a craggy, masculine face he thought, almost handsome.

He'd have to quit his job of course, but then there was more to life than being a ranch foreman on Southfork Ranch. Besides, with experience like that, he could go anywhere. Maybe he would take Sue Ellen to Odessa and buy a little house—he had the savings. Maybe she wouldn't have all the luxury she had now, he thought, but she sure as heck would never be starved for love again. He would see to that personally. And last night, when he brought her into his humble rooms, hadn't she told him she wished she had a little house just like it so that she could leave that big mansion and all the unhappiness inside it?

Maybe thinking about getting a house for her was rushing things, Ray thought, but he had to be prepared. J.R. could return tonight and come looking to kill him. If he did, Ray knew exactly what he'd say and do. "J.R, you can thank yourself for this whole mess," he'd say, looking the bastard straight in the eye. "You neglected your wife so she came to me. But, see, Sue Ellen is a fine woman. She deserves a helluva lot better than a rat bastard like you, and I'm going to see to it that she gets it." Then, if J.R. wanted to fight it out, fine. J.R. wasn't as strong as he thought he was anyway.

* * *

Sue Ellen sat by the pool, her dark glasses securely in place so that the bright morning rays wouldn't hit her sensitive eyes. It was past ten. The maid told her that J.R. had come home earlier, had had breakfast with Jock and Ellie, and had left for the office while she slept off the remains of last night's drinking. It was just as well she hadn't seen him this morning, Sue Ellen thought, trying to let the healing rays of the sun penetrate her very bruised soul.

More and more, J.R. had been accusing her of drinking too much and she wouldn't have wanted him to see her with a hangover this morning. Just remembering how she stood in the driveway yelling last night made her shiver with revulsion. What had she said, she wondered, as she reached for the juice Raoul had put beside her.

She couldn't remember; the alcohol had blocked out the details, but she was sure her behavior had been unbecoming of a Southern lady.

When J.R. came home tonight, she would beg for his forgiveness. Meanwhile, she made a solemn vow to God never, ever, ever to drink so much again.

Ray Krebbs came out of his house dressed in a neatly washed and ironed cotton plaid shirt, the sweet scent of men's cologne wafting around his face. Instead of turning toward the stables, he strode confidently toward the mansion.

He saw her from across the lawn. She was lying on chaise-longue in a royal blue bathing suit, wearing a white, wide-brimmed hat, her tanned and curvy legs comfortably crossed. She was so beautiful that for a moment, he thought it was all too good to be true. But Sue Ellen had been very clear last night. The love she had been holding inside for him so long had burst like a dam and flooded them both with a kind of dangerous happiness. Just looking at her again, now, reminded him again. She lifted her lovely head in his direction and Ray felt his body responding. She was smiling at him—that wide, generous smile of hers—a smile that said, "Yes."

Ray's pace quickened as he walked to the pool. She had turned back to a magazine on her lap. She must not have realized he was coming to talk to her, to tell her that they would leave tonight if she was willing, to tell her he loved her and that he would stand beside her no matter how hard the Ewings might fight against their love. Last night, he had not said those words to her. He had been too caught up in her confession to respond in kind. Only his body had spoken last night with a sensual eloquence one wouldn't associate with the staid and steady ranch foreman.

Walking around the pool Ray quietly went behind her chair and put his sunburned hands firmly on her shoulders. "Sue Ellen . . ." he murmured, "good morning, sweetheart." He bent down to kiss her, but the shocked look on her face under her sun hat stunned him. He froze in place.

"Ray Krebbs, what has gotten into you?" she said as if she were offended. "How dare you put your hands on me. How dare you?" Was she joking, he wondered? She was treating him as if last night had never happened.

"Honey, Sue Ellen, what's the matter? What happened?" he asked, his heart beating wildly.

"My name is *Mrs. Ewing*, Ray. You should know that by now!" she answered uncomfortably.

"Even after last night, 'Mrs. Ewing'?" he asked, trying to be light. She *had* to be joking, he thought in panic.

Sue Ellen looked alarmed for just a second and then shook her head lightly. "I haven't the faintest idea what you're talking about, but I do believe my husband and his father would be very upset to hear that you were hanging around the pool bothering me during your working hours."

And with that, she picked up the magazine that was lying on her lap and pretended to turn her attention to a crossword puzzle.

Ray stood by the pool for a moment as if he had just been shot. Then, turning to hide the stinging in his eyes, he began walking to the stables as he did every other day of his life.

After he left, Sue Ellen planned her day. She had to save her marriage and she had to save herself. Today she would take action. She was not powerless, she reminded herself, echoing the pyschologist's advice to her. She was *not* powerless. But, she couldn't wait for someone to come and save her—she had to act!

Pam left the medical center and headed toward her car, a ten-year-old blue Ford she had driven as a single woman. From across the busy street she saw it and smiled. When she was single, the car had been like a reliable old friend, but recently she realized the car was just a vehicle, a means of getting from one place to another, and an unattractive one at that. Even here on the streets of Dallas it looked somehow out of place. Maybe, she thought, she would stop at a car wash on her way home; maybe a good wash and wax job would help.

Last week Bobby had teased her unmercifully about the car when it was parked in the Ewing driveway next to his and J.R.'s brand new Mercedes. She had had to giggle at the fun he made of it. He called it a mutt among thoroughbreds. And though she had said nothing, she thought with amusement that the old, blue car was a little like herself in relation to the Ewings.

The breeze was so cooling and the sun so warm that Pamela looked up at the sky for a moment as if greeting an old friend. She couldn't help but feel wonderful. Her entire life was going so well, she thought, as a rush of childlike happiness swept through her body. Her marriage to Bobby, which everyone in Dallas had predicted would fail, was strong and secure. Instead of diminishing their love, marriage had actually strengthened it. And Bobby's readiness to have a baby, while it didn't exactly match her internal schedule, was touching to her. It was evidence that her marriage would last. Pam felt that she was one of the lucky ones who would have a stable love to build her life on.

Today, her visit to Dr. Wagner gave her reason to be happy, too. The kindly old man had told her she was completely healthy and fully recovered from the disastrous miscarriage she'd had when she and Bobby were first married. That pregnancy had been an unplanned surprise, and though she and Bobby had accepted it, neither one was truly ready for it. But now she could begin a family whenever she wished.

Pam had sighed with relief when the doctor had given her the news. It was as if a weight had been lifted from her shoulders. How much of her reluctance to try to become pregnant now had to do with that unhappy experience, she wondered quickly, but then she put the thought out of her mind. Even a year later the thought of that whole episode hurt her terribly.

It was best to wait. In a year or two she would not be much older, but she intended to be much wiser about facing motherhood. She would use the time to read and observe and learn about the art of good mothering so that she would give her child the best possible start in life. But right now, she was lonely for the girls at The Store where she had worked as a buyer for over five years. And Liz Craig, her old boss and good friend, was on a campaign to bring her back. It was flattering to be needed and maybe after she worked for a year, she'd be ready for motherhood. Maybe she wouldn't even wait that long. But in any case, there was no need to rush. Bobby was willing to be patient, albeit with some reluctance, and everything was right in the world.

Pam stopped at the crossing, her car keys in hand. She noticed a familiar car pull up to the curb to park. At first she wasn't sure, but then she realized it was her sister-in-law.

"Sue Ellen!" Pam cried. "Hello!"

Sue Ellen smiled as widely as she could and gave her sister-in-law a little wave. Smiling broadly had been her habitual reaction to emotional discomfort for so long that it had almost become a part of her personality. But the last person she wanted to see now was her sister-in-law, Pamela Ewing.

Sue Ellen had tried to hide her distaste for her new sister-in-law behind a chummy exterior ever since Bobby brought the girl home. She invited her to Daughters of the Alamo meetings and on shopping excursions—most of which the other woman declined. But even this false show of friendliness was getting harder and harder.

Pam was always so cheerful, so full of happiness and compassion. Sue Ellen could tell by the look in her eyes that Pam secretly felt sorry for her, and it made her furious to have to be the object of pity. Now, just when she most wanted to be alone, here was Pam grinning from ear to ear. She seems so tickled, Sue Ellen thought, just to see a familiar face downtown, as if running into a friendly face was such a big event. Sue Ellen stepped from the car, her mind working as fast as it could. What could she possibly tell Pam that would get rid of her as soon as possible?

"What a coincidence! I was here for a doctor's appointment. If I knew you were coming into town I would have offered you a lift."

The mere thought of riding anywhere in Pamela's old car had no appeal whatsoever for Sue Ellen who would not have been caught dead in her sister-in-law's ancient, beat-up jalopy. She couldn't understand Pamela's attachment to it.

"Oh, that's all right. I had a few errands," was Sue Ellen's friendly sounding reply.

"Well, what are you doing here?" Pam asked unaware of the invasion of privacy Sue Ellen took her question to be.

Sue Ellen hesitated. She needed a lie. Not a big black one, but a medium-sized grey one. One that would throw her sister-in-law in the wrong direction. What she was about to do required the utmost secrecy. If anyone from the family found out about it, especially J.R., her entire plan would fall to ashes. Pamela simply could not be trusted at a time like this.

"Well, I have a doctor's appointment myself. Isn't that a coincidence?" Sue Ellen said, hesitantly.

"Nothing serious, I hope," Pam responded, that look of compassion entering her eyes in just the way Sue Ellen abhorred.

"Oh, no," Sue Ellen assured her. "It's just time for my yearly physical."

Pam finally sensed something was up, but she just wasn't close enough to Sue Ellen to challenge her answers. She distinctly remembered Sue Ellen having her physical just one month ago. A worried look passed over her face. Could Sue Ellen be sick? Or was she worried about something? Maybe some friendly interest was called for.

"Would you like me to wait for you? We could have lunch together if you like. I'm free for the whole afternoon." Pam's offer was sincere. She would have liked nothing better than to have Sue Ellen as a friend and an ally. J.R. had tried many times to hurt Pam and drive her from the family, but she didn't hold that against his wife. Sue Ellen was more of a mystery to Pam. Sometimes she seemed warm and sensitive, other times, cold and haughty. But maybe the latter qualities were just her way of defending herself from the difficult burden of being J.R.'s wife. In any case, Pam found Sue Ellen intriguing. She would have liked to get to know her better—woman to woman—away from the family.

Sue Ellen coughed uncomfortably. Would Pam never take the hint?

"Well, I'd love to have lunch, Pam, but I . . . I'm meeting J.R." It was a lovely lie. Having lunch with J.R. was something she would have liked to do so many times when they were first married. Even now she could imagine them talking sincerely over lunch like other married people, clearing the air, forgiving each other, vowing to do better. It was all a fantasy, of course, but a noble one.

"Well, okay then. See you later."

"Yes. See you tonight, and thanks for the invitation. We'll do it another time."

"Sure." And with that, Pamela walked across the street and stepped into her car.

Sue Ellen stood on the street waving until Pam's car was entirely out of view. She didn't want Pam to look into her mirror and see her turning away from the medical center and walking to the old brick building on the corner. As she walked into the lobby, she pulled up the collar of her thin beige raincoat and looked around for any other people she might know. Fortunately, there was no one.

The adoption offices were drab. Instead of a warm colorful decor, the place had a pseudo-corporate look to it with drab green plastic covering the tattered office chairs. Cheap prints of country scenes hung on the wall in frames without glass. With only the briefest glance, the receptionist told Sue Ellen to have a seat.

The seats in the waiting room were made of cracked imitation leather. Sue Ellen checked to see that her stockings didn't get snagged on the frayed edges of the chair as she sat. So this was it: Brentwood Adoption Services. Sue Ellen picked up a copy of a two-month-old issue of *Mothers Today*. There was nothing in it that interested her in the least. An old *People* magazine had little for her to read as well. She leafed through the magazine nervously, stopping only momentarily for provocative photos and interesting quotes.

Opening her handbag, she took out a mirror and applied a fresh coat of red lipstick to her mouth. Bright colors looked good on Sue Ellen, and she used them to her advantage. This morning in particular she wanted to make the best possible impression. She had gotten up that morning with a mean hangover, but a shower and some eyedrops and a little splash of wine in her juice had helped her to get over that sick feeling.

Sitting there waiting, Sue Ellen had the odd sensation of being a schoolgirl about to take a test. Her palms began to sweat profusely. She tried using the technique a psychologist had once suggested for moments like this, and internally ordered herself to calm down. It didn't work.

What if they didn't accept her, she thought in panic?

But then, her thoughts countered, they *had* to accept her—she was one of the wealthiest women in the state. They couldn't possibly refuse her. Or could they?

After what seemed like hours, a young, dark-haired woman appeared in the doorway and asked in a friendly tone for Mrs. Ewing. Sue Ellen sat bolt upright, a charge of electricity jolting through her body. She responded with as much presence as she could, "Yes." She didn't want to seem too eager. She didn't want to seem anxious. She didn't want to seem desperate—but she was all of those things, and despite her best efforts they all showed.

Barbara Walsh was used to dealing with nervous people. As a social worker she had seen it all, though she was still in her twenties. Mrs Ewing was no worse than most who came to her.

"Mrs. Ewing, how may we help you?" she asked, when the women reached her small, windowless office.

Sue Ellen's eyes found the social worker's. She spoke with a firm voice tinged with vulnerability. "Why, I would like to adopt a baby as soon as possible."

"Are you married, Mrs. Ewing?"

Sue Ellen looked astonished at the question. "Why, of course I'm married!"

The social worker smiled. "Well, you know, not everyone who wants to adopt a child is married these days, and you didn't mention your husband. Is he in favor of your adopting a child as well?"

Sue Ellen smiled nervously. Her voice dropped in volume as she lied. "Oh, yes. Of course. He just happens to be a very busy man. That's why he couldn't be here today."

Barbara Walsh's eyes lit up. Ewing. She hadn't thought of it when she first met the attractive brunette sitting in front of her.

"Mrs. Ewing—is your family the Ewing family of Ewing Oil?"

Again Sue Ellen smiled nervously. "Yes, it is. But I hope you won't hold that against me," she said trying to banter comfortably as she suspected men did when they made business deals.

It worked. The social worker was laughing. "Oh,

no! I should say not. In fact, quite the opposite. We are very concerned that our adoptive parents have the necessary material means to provide a good home for our children. In your case, I imagine, there would be no problem."

Sue Ellen smiled happily like a child at a fair. It was her first genuine smile of the day.

"Oh, no, we're quite . . . comfortable."

"Of course, money isn't the first consideration. There's also the matter of love, as well as time and energy," Miss Walsh said.

Sue Ellen's head was bobbing up and down, agreeing with every word the social worker said. She wanted Miss Walsh to know she agreed wholeheartedly with those ideas. And beyond that, she found the social worker's words oddly comforting. Time, love, energy—weren't those the very things she most wanted to share with a baby? And just because she wanted to get a child before Pam did and become the favored daughter-in-law didn't mean she would be any less loving.

"Oh, yes," she said, after Miss Walsh stopped talking. "More than anything else in the world, I want—we want to share our home and our love with a child. My husband and I have a very deep and loving relationship and we both want to share our lives with a child. It's very important to us."

It sounded so wonderful, Sue Ellen thought mindlessly—and maybe it was still possible. J.R. had loved her once. Maybe a child would bring them closer. Last night after their horrible scene, she had blamed herself for his leaving. He had every right, she thought, when she woke up with a stiff hangover. The whole night was a kind of crazy blur.

But maybe after the baby came, J.R. would stay home and she'd stop drinking. Maybe when they watched their baby walk for the first time he would sweep her up in his arms and kiss her and tell her he was crazy to have ever looked at another girl.

"Mrs. Ewing! Excuse me. Are you feeling all right? You look a little faint."

"No, no. It's just, well, I got a new prescription for glasses that I use when I drive and I have a teeny little headache. That's all. Now, you were saying you do have a child for us then?"

"Yes. I'm sure your application will be approved, and we have a lovely three-and-a-half-year-old boy, Carmen Alvarez. He is a bright—"

Sue Ellen looked confused. "Three-and-a-half? Why, that's much too old! I want a baby! A little tiny baby."

Miss Walsh had seen and heard this all before, many times. She began her usual speech. "Mrs. Ewing, perhaps you don't understand. Legal abortion has changed the face of adoption in our nation. Adopting a small baby will take a long time, if there is one available. Unless, that is, you'd be willing to take a handicapped baby. We do have them on occasion. But even a handicapped child would take about two years to get. I can't give you any idea of when we might have an infant for you"

Sue Ellen looked around her and for the first time she noticed how shabby the adoption office really was. She lifted her hand from the wooden arm of the chair she sat in. Her hand felt dirty. She would say it once more until this stupid woman understood.

"My husband and I want to adopt a healthy Caucasian baby. Now we have money enough to provide that baby with every possible comfort and an excellent education. I do not see what the problem is."

"The problem, Mrs. Ewing, is that babies like the one you describe are not available for adoption unless you are willing to wait oh, say, three to eight years."

By then, Pamela's children would be in school, Sue Ellen thought. A wave of nausea came over her. It was a desperate feeling, a feeling that everything she touched turned to dust, that any effort she made to help herself was just so much wasted energy. She slumped into her chair and said weakly, "I can't wait that long. I want a baby. I want a little baby and I can't wait."

Pitiful tears poured down the cheeks of the former beauty queen. Her life was falling apart and there was nothing she could do about it.

Miss Walsh handed her a fresh tissue. "Please, Mrs. Ewing. I'm sure something can be worked out."

The woman in front of her was crying as if her heart was breaking. A colleague peeked in through the door to see what was happening and the social worker waved her away.

She would do something she seldom did. She knew a lawyer who sometimes arranged private adoptions. It was an arduous and expensive process, but maybe in this case it would help. Money obviously wouldn't be a problem for the Ewings. There might be a girl—a college student perhaps—who would be willing to trade her unwanted newborn baby for a pile of money. She had known of a couple of cases where it had worked out for everybody concerned. And despite her desperation, Mrs. Ewing seemed like a warm person. She really did seem to want a baby to love.

"I don't usually do this, but here," she said reaching into her desk and pulling out a small white business card. "This is a lawyer who arranges . . . private adoptions. Please don't tell anyone I gave you his number or I could get into a lot of trouble and lose my job. Private adoption is frowned upon by the agency, but sometimes it can provide a couple with a baby when the ordinary processes fail."

"Private adoption" sometimes meant black market baby. The difference between them might be only a thin line and one that neither Barbara Walsh or Sue Ellen Ewing wanted to look at at the moment.

Sue Ellen's tears turned from desperation to gratitude as she stood up and took the card from the social worker's hand. "Thank you, thank you," she said over and over. "I will never forget your kindness, Miss Walsh."

Chapter Eight

The sun was beating down on the range with a brutal force. Only the Texas bluebells, the small wildflowers that flourished under the blazing sun, were unaffected by the heat. For the men and animals on the range, the sun was killing.

Ordinarily, Ray and Bobby would have hauled themselves back to the ranch to stay under cover until the heat of the day passed. But out on the back four hundred, a steer had broken its leg when a fox ran across its path. The two men had to stay with the animal until the vet could get there.

Ray looked up at the big blue Texas sky, his eyes squinting from the force of the sun, and sighed wearily as he brushed the scent of the animal off his hands.

"Ever just feel like taking off and never coming back?" he asked spontaneously. "Just going as far away from things as you can and not turning back?"

Bobby looked at Ray in amazement and laughed softly. "Are you kidding? Ray, you're talking to a man who spent years running away from things. It seems to me I've just learned how good it is to stay in one place! I'm not going anywhere!"

Ray went on, still looking at the sky, almost as if he hadn't heard Bobby. "Well, I'm going to take off one day soon. You know, I've always wanted to get up to Calgary and maybe check out that rodeo. I always thought I could maybe make it as a manager on the riding circuit. And it would sure beat the hell out of staying here and just getting older every day."

Bobby wondered when and why Ray had become so dissatisfied at Southfork—he had always seemed so happy with his job. It seemed unlikely, but maybe Krebbs hadn't got enough of a raise last year. Bobby made a mental note to discuss the situation with Jock one night soon. Losing a foreman like Ray Krebbs would be a terrible blow to the operation of Southfork Ranch, and Bobby wanted to do everything in his power to make sure the foreman stayed and was happy.

Suddenly, a palomino came riding across the range creating a cloud of dust in its way. Pam was riding the horse, her russet hair waving in the wind.

"Pam!" Bobby cried, good naturedly. "Just in time! We need somebody to help us pick up this baby and put him in the truck," he said, referring to the steer who lay comfortably on his side.

Pam smiled and stuck out her tongue impishly. "No dice, sailor," was her reply. "I just came to see if I could borrow your car. Mine is out, I think it's the radiator—that or the engine—I can't tell."

"Or the transmission, or the starter, or the carburetor, or the valves . . ." Bobby said, teasing her. "When that car goes, watch out! It may explode!"

"Very funny. But I plan to have it fixed tomorrow. I just need a car now to go to town. I decided to take the job, and Liz asked me to come out for a meeting they're having with the owners."

"You're taking the job? I thought you were going to think about that some more!" Bobby said forcefully with an edge of anger in his voice. The playfulness of their exchange was over. Bobby's mood changed to one of dead-seriousness.

"Well, I *did* think about it. And I'm going to take it," Pamela told him evenly.

"Women. Who can understand them? Can you, Ray?" Bobby said, trying to hide his rage. He expected a smile or a laugh from the good-natured foreman. But instead Ray turned away and shook his head vigorously from side to side.

"Don't talk to me about women, Bobby," he said with bitterness in his voice. "I don't know the first thing about them, they don't know the first thing about me, and that's the way I intend to keep it. As far as I can tell, they're not worth the effort it takes to be with them."

Pamela looked at the foreman with a surprised and hurt look on her face.

"Oh, not all of 'em. Not you, Pam," he mumbled diplomatically. "Just ninety-nine-and-a-half percent!" Then, without looking at either of them, he turned his attention back to the steer.

Bobby looked at Pam. There was no sense in arguing about it anymore. He shook his head hopelessly and muttered, "Sure. Take the car. You're going to do what you want anyway, aren't you?"

Pam decided it was best not to respond to that

question. She took the car keys he held out to her and mounted the horse for the return ride to the ranch.

Lucy answered the phone to hear a friendly, masculine voice ask for Mrs. Ewing. When Lucy asked him which Mrs. Ewing he meant, he had said flirtatiously, "Why, I mean Sue Ellen, honey." The man sounded "cute," Lucy thought.

When Sue Ellen rushed into the den to take the call, Lucy found herself lingering to listen. The conversation was short but tantalizing to Lucy who read into it all sorts of undertones.

"Hello—, oh, yes." Sue Ellen breathed into the receiver in her best humble Miss Texas tone. "I'm surprised you called so quickly, I just left the message. Well, I just got back from downtown but I suppose I could run in if it means we could meet. No, I don't want to wait, either. The Cowboy Boot on San Antonio. Fine. I'll be there."

As Sue Ellen hung up, Lucy looked at her with a knowing grin. Nothing would have pleased the girl more than believing that Sue Ellen was dating another man. In her opinion, it was exactly what J.R. deserved!

J.R. had driven Lucy's mother, Valene, and her father, Gary, from Southfork when Lucy was just a baby. Apparently, J.R. didn't approve of the fact that his brother had come home with a waitress and was determined to break up the young couple. Unfortunately, he succeeded. First, he managed to drive Gary away and then he threatened Valene, telling her that if she didn't go he would make her life miserable. Worst of all, he forced Valene to leave her little baby girl behind for his mother and father to raise, convincing her she was too poor to bring up the child on her own.

For the sake of her daughter, Valene had gone along with J.R. But later, when she realized her life would be ruined if she could not raise her little daughter, she'd come back for the child. J.R. was waiting for her. He threatened her life and told her to leave the state of Texas if she knew what was best for her. Lucy had had to accept Jock and Ellie as her parents rather than her grandparents.

As Lucy had gotten a little older and had been able to piece together the story of what J.R. had done to her mother and father, she vowed she would get her revenge one day. But now she had to be content with *little* pleasures—like hoping he and Sue Ellen were miserable together and hoping that Sue Ellen would find herself a boyfriend.

"Well, well, Sue Ellen. He sure sounded sexy," Lucy remarked, trying to appear casual but with a hint of intensity in her voice.

"Lucy!" chided Sue Ellen in her best Daughters of the Alamo tone.

"Meeting him this afternoon, huh? You both must be very anxious. You sure were foxy on the phone," the teenager went on, taunting her aunt further.

"Lucy, the man I was talking to happens to be a lawyer! In fact, I have never even met him. But I *do* have a little legal business to discuss with him, if you don't mind. It happens to be a perfectly innocent matter."

"And does Uncle J.R. know about your little legal business? I thought he had a whole staff of lawyers to take care of that stuff."

Sue Ellen went pale. Lucy had hit a nerve. Sue Ellen had been married to J.R. long enough to know that he would destroy her plans if he found out about them before they were complete. She had to present him with a *fait accompli*. It was the only way. Otherwise she might never get what she wanted and needed so much. And all it would take was a little slip of the tongue by Lucy to destroy her. She had to do something and quick. Grabbing Lucy at the wrist firmly, in an uncharacteristic way, Sue Ellen looked deeply into the girl's eyes as she issued the threat.

"No, he doesn't know a thing about it. And if he finds out I will know who told him, and believe me, Lucy, you will be one sorry girl."

Lucy was baffled. Then, a smile spread across her face. "You mean you're finally getting smart, Sue Ellen? Are you going to discuss getting a divorce from J.R.?"

"Believe whatever you want, Lucy—but don't you dare breathe a word of this to J.R. or anyone else! Believe me! You'll regret it if you do!"

"Gosh, Sue Ellen—this new boyfriend of yours must be quite a guy!" Lucy retorted fearlessly.

Sue Ellen was fed up with Lucy's impudence, but rather than confront the girl any more, she left the room. She didn't need anyone's opinions about her marriage—especially not those of her teenage niece.

The Cowboy Boot was just on the edge of the Dallas business district, a few blocks west of the canal. It was a restaurant that catered to the not-yet crowd: men who were not yet wealthy enough for the Cattleman's Club, and secretaries who had not yet found husbands.

Cliff Barnes had been coming here for years because the food was served in generous portions at unbeatable prices. Additionally, the maitre'd knew him and respectfully called him "Mr. Barnes," something that gave Cliff a little thrill whenever he walked through the swinging doors.

Today Cliff had a meeting with one of the county assessors, a man by the name of Sol Rubin. Rubin's opinions about politics were both informed and powerful. And since Cliff was on the verge of announcing his intentions to run for state senator, he hoped Rubin would be willing to give him some valuable information and support. Cliff's eyes danced around the crowded dining room. There was no sign of Rubin yet.

Suddenly Barnes felt a hard slap on his back as a loud male voice cried out, "Well, if it ain't Cliff Barnes!" Buzz Connors, an old law school classmate of Cliff's, was standing beside him, grinning from ear to ear like a car salesman about to make a sale.

"Hey, Buzz—how are you?" Cliff asked politely, while looking around the room in the hopes that Sol Rubin wouldn't see him with Connors. Bill "Buzz" Connors had made his reputation as a lawyer in Dallas by handling the cases other lawyers turned down. His practice consisted mostly of "ambulance-chasing" and some private adoptions. Cliff had it on good information that Connors actually attended the funerals of complete strangers so that he could pass out his card to the bereaved after the ceremonies just to drum up some business for himself.

As for private adoptions, these sometimes semi-legal arrangements were frowned upon by most knowledgeable members of the Dallas legal community. While they weren't strictly illegal, they were frequently far from being acceptable. Often the biological mothers would come back years later to claim the children who had been supposedly "adopted" years before. And the courts usually sided with them. What that amounted to was the court's blessing on the biological mothers and a blow to the adoptive parents. It was a way of telling the community at large just how the law viewed these adoptions. This unfortunate situation caused heartbreak and confusion all around.

"So, buddy," Buzz was asking, "what brings you out to this neck of the woods?" Even in law school, Connors had had a particularly annoying way of expressing himself almost exclusively in clichés. The Cowboy Boot was located off a busy street, after all. It was hardly in the woods.

"Meeting a fellow to discuss the state senate campaign," Cliff replied truthfully while revealing as little as possible.

"Yes," Buzz said, almost shouting, as Cliff stood beside him hanging his head in embarrassment. "I heard you were going to run for public office! That's something! Really something! Imagine me having a big shot friend in Austin!"

Cliff was trying to turn his body in a way that wouldn't offend Buzz, but that would cast doubt on whether he was talking to Buzz or to a perfect stranger standing next to him by the cigarette machine.

"Oh, I may run. May not," Cliff mumbled, almost incoherently. The truth was he planned to declare his candidacy later in the week. But now, he desperately wanted to throw Connors off track lest his school chum started bragging about knowing the candidate personally, and therefore costing him precious votes. But Buzz was undaunted.

"Say Cliff," he said in a loud whisper, his voice turned suddenly serious, "can you help me out a little when you get to the big time?"

Cliff was squirming. He hadn't even announced his campaign and already this guy was asking for favors. What was the best response in a case like this? If he straightforwardly refused he would be apt to make an enemy of Connors. And Cliff knew he couldn't afford any enemies if he was going to oppose the favored candidate of the Ewings and their powerful oil industry friends.

On the other hand, if he said yes he was opening himself up to corruption before he had even taken office!

Suddenly, Cliff was struck with an inspiration. He looked at Buzz with surprise and then burst out with a loud and raucous laugh. "Very good, fella! Excellent!" he roared as if his old classmate had just told him the funniest joke in the entire history of man.

It worked. Buzz looked bewildered for a moment and then began laughing, too, as if enjoying his own joke.

Just then, Sue Ellen appeared in the doorway looking especially beautiful in a dark red dress that clung to her. She looked frightened and vulnerable as her darting brown eyes searched the crowded room. Connors had only told her, laughingly, to look for the handsomest man in the room wearing a grey suit. That, he assured her, would be him.

Since Cliff had kept an eye on the entrance, he noticed Sue Ellen immediately. She was a vision of beauty.

Ever since he had first set eyes on his sister-in-law by marriage, he had felt a powerful attraction to her. She was a stunning woman, but beyond that she came perilously close to representing Cliff's ideal—a warm, voluptuous brunette.

Since he had been a kid, a woman like Sue Ellen had dominated his dreams, making the real women he met seem unattractive. And while he didn't really believe in "love at first sight," his attraction to her was powerful enough to make him reconsider the notion. Now there she was, standing alone. She looked as though she were just waiting for someone to go to her, smile at her, help her . . .

"That's my sister-in-law," Cliff said in an almost worshipful tone.

"Oh, good," Buzz said turning and calling to her. "Mrs. Ewing! Buzz Connors here!"

As Sue Ellen made her way through the room, Cliff turned to Buzz, a look of disbelief on his face.

"How do you know Sue Ellen?" he asked Buzz. Why would *any* Ewing be associated with a sleazy lawyer like Buzz Connors, he thought? It didn't make sense.

"Well, Cliff," Buzz answered, enjoying the mystery of the moment, "let's just say she's a client of mine, but that her business with me is strictly a confidential matter. Okay?"

When Sue Ellen reached the two men she felt the same pull toward Cliff that he felt for her. She, too, had felt the power of attraction when they had first met. How odd, she thought, as she stood politely saying hello to him, that she would find Cliff Barnes, her husband's arch enemy, so completely charming. Was it simply the lure of forbidden fruit? Sue Ellen didn't think so. Cliff was as charming and sweet as a man could be.

When Buzz suggested they take a table, Sue Ellen put her hand out to Barnes who held it gently in his own for a moment longer than the bounds of a perfunctory handshake. His touch sent a warm thrill through her, but she pulled her hand away quickly, trying to deny the feeling to herself. She turned away from him and walked to the table in the back of the restaurant with Buzz Connors.

"*He* doesn't know, does he?" were her first worried words to her new lawyer. "Cliff is my sister-in-law's brother and she could ruin me if she knew!"

"Mrs. Ewing! Mr. Barnes is a lawyer himself and he fully understands the confidentiality of our relationship. Of course he doesn't know. No one knows, except you and me."

Sue Ellen breathed easier as she settled into her chair.

"Now," he said in a businesslike tone, "I've taken the liberty of drawing up the necessary papers . . ."

Sue Ellen was shocked. "Papers? But I'm not ready to sign anything. I'm just here to talk. Besides, I thought buying a baby was illegal."

Buzz leaned back in his chair and smiled. He had heard this many times before and he knew the proper response.

"Well, Mrs. Ewing, what it comes down to, after everything is said and done, is whether you want a baby or not! A private adoption may not be fully sanctioned by the law but, on the other hand, there's no law against it! And there *are* those girls who don't want to have an abortion or go through the red tape that an adoption agency would put them through. For them, a private adoption is ideal.'' He didn't add that it gave them cash when they needed it most and allowed for the option of changing their minds in the future. "Of course, this method isn't for everybody. It happens to be very expensive. But, in your case, I suppose that's not a significant factor.''

"How much will it cost?'' Sue Ellen wanted to know.

"Twenty thousand dollars,'' he said, quickly adding the list of reasons for the high cost. "You understand, there are the girl's medical expenses, and of course, she needs a place to stay, and my fees, the hospital . . .''

While he went on, Sue Ellen's head was spinning. She was a wealthy woman, but J.R. still had access to the money in a way that she didn't. She would have to use her credit and tell J.R. she had spent the money on clothes for herself. That way he would never miss the money. She'd say she wanted all new things from the best new Japanese designers, and she'd make sure she had a few outfits that would really impress him. J.R. never gave her an argument when she was spending money on clothes. He liked her to look good, and it was something he was willing to pay for.

"How soon can I get my baby?'' was the next information she wanted to learn from him.

"Well,'' was the reply, "there's a girl who's seven

months pregnant and really has no money at all. Her family abandoned her and she's all alone living right here in Dallas."

"I want to meet her," Sue Ellen cut in.

"Oh, Mrs. Ewing, that's a poor idea. I speak from experience when I say that meeting the biological mother can be upsetting and . . ."

"Mr. Connors, if I am spending twenty thousand dollars, I feel I have a right to meet the girl. I don't want to make any mistakes. I'm sure you can appreciate that."

Sue Ellen was proud of herself for saying it so firmly. As for Connors, he could hardly argue with her. Reluctantly, he took a small piece of paper from his jacket and wrote down the address.

Rita Briggs was lying on the bed exhausted when the phone rang. Not many people had her number in Dallas, and she could count on the call being from one of three people. One was her welfare worker, a dense, pimply-faced nerd who was doing the best he could to hold up her checks as far as she could tell, even though he kept telling her he was trying to get them for her as fast as possible. Or it could be Garbo, a gay runaway she had met a few weeks ago. He had taken to her like a puppy and she was trying to get rid of him. There wasn't any room in her life for friends. Or it could be the lawyer, the one who told her he might be able to get her two thousand bucks if she was willing to sell the baby she was carrying.

Rita reached across the bed for her cigarettes while the phone continued to ring. She had to have a smoke before she could talk to any one of them.

Taking one and placing the pack on her swollen belly, she struck a match and reached for the phone.

"Yeah?" she inquired roughly.

It was the lawyer. He had a prospect.

When she had first found out she was pregnant, Rita had been scared but secretly happy. She had ignored the missed periods and swelling belly until several months had gone by. But then there was no denying it. When she gave it a little thought, it had seemed to her that being pregnant would mean there was no way her parents could stop her from marrying Eddie. Her mother had cried and her father had slapped her, but what could they do? When Eddie came over that night, they didn't throw him out. They talked about a wedding instead. Rita was glowing with happiness inside though she didn't want her parents or Eddie to see how thrilled she really was. Being thrilled was definitely uncool, and Rita had a reputation to protect.

She and Eddie decided to get married by the Justice of the Peace. Her mother didn't want it all to be cut and dry, so they chose to wait a couple of weeks so that Rita could get a nice dress and shoes. Her father even told them he'd spring for some flowers and a little party afterwards in her Aunt Louise's basement.

Eddie didn't look exactly tickled, but then, what guy was before his wedding? He'd adjust, her mother told her when he left. And he probably would have, too, except that he decided to have his own little celebration with a few of his friends three nights before the wedding. Somebody thought it would be fun to hold up the supermarket a few blocks away so that the groom would have a few bucks to throw away on his Atlantic City honeymoon.

Rita found out the next day when her landlady asked her if she heard about the shooting. The landlady was grinning ear to ear about the three punks who were shot and killed by the store manager. He was tired of having his store ripped-off and so he had been prepared. "Thank God," said the landlady, "for once it wasn't an owner or a clerk or, God-forbid, some innocent customer."

The local paper confirmed Rita's worst fears with a picture of her blood-spattered boyfriend being rushed to the local hospital, dead on arrival. So much for the wedding and so much for the baby. If Rita could have had the kid aborted then, she would have, but no doctor, no matter how liberal, would abort a six-month-old fetus. When she told her parents she thought Eddie was right to try and stick it to the supermarket guy so she and he had some dough, they had flown into a rage and thrown her out of the house.

Well, she got back at them for that. Instead of staying away for a night with her aunt like they wanted her to, she took off for Dallas and had no intention of ever going home again. Let them worry about her. Who the hell were they to her anyway? Just her parents who she didn't need anymore anyway.

Once before, when she had first moved to Dallas, Sue Ellen had gotten lost while driving home from a dental appointment and had passed through this neighborhood. At the time, she had been horrified by the poverty around her—the broken bottles that

littered the streets, fast food restaurants' paper bags
that blew along the sidewalks when a breeze came.

But worst of all was the sight of the children, so
many of them dirty-faced, poorly clothed angels
who played on the streets in spite of the traffic
around them and the sirens going off in their ears.
Ignorant of the wealthy world around them, they
would grow up and continue the cycle. The men
who sat on the stoops of old buildings drinking from
bottles covered by brown paper bags were once
children here. And the bloated women carrying
shopping bags filled with rags and other junky
treasures were, too.

It was depressing for Sue Ellen to see people
living like this. When she was growing up she had
known places like this, but now it all seemed like a
distant dirty world, a world she wished didn't exist.
And if she had a chance to help somebody *out* of this
world, she wanted to do it.

The address on the paper was "247 Elm." Sue
Ellen looked up at the run-down apartment house
where an old woman looked out from an upper story
window watching everything with bitter eyes.

The apartment doorbells were broken as was the
lock on the front door, so Sue Ellen walked in,
gasping at the smell of feline urine that filled the
dark hallway. Climbing up the creaking wooden
steps, she paused to get a handkerchief to cover her
nose. The scent of her own fine French perfume
provided her with a welcome relief. Climbing the
stairs she thought of her suite at Southfork and
counted it as a blessing.

"Number 48," the door said corresponding to
the paper. The door was painted dark green but

gashes in the paint revealed a history of red, brown, black, and beige. Sue Ellen hesitated for a second, gathering her courage, then knocked lightly.

Chapter Nine

Rita Briggs approached the door slowly, an irrational anger simmering within her. All her life she had needed money and now there was a woman on the other side who had so much of it that she could afford to buy a baby—Rita's baby.

Money. It made a difference between having the life you wanted, or having a life filled with drudgery and hard times. As a child she'd seen her parents' marriage falling apart whenever the subject of money came up. In school she'd known kids too poor to eat properly. Maybe if *she* had had money she would have made something of herself instead of being an eighteen-year-old loser. She had had the looks, that was for sure. Before her belly started sticking out, she'd had an eye-catching figure and a face to match. She could have been a model— maybe a movie star—*something*.

Rita had gone to the priest a couple weeks before she left home and he told her she wasn't thinking right. "You're young," he had told her in the encouraging tone of voice that said he couldn't possibly know what was really happening. "You're young. And if you work hard, you can go back to school. There are scholarships if you're willing to work."

The guy was talking as if he lived on another planet! Scholarships? Rita could just about read! She still had to sound out the words whenever she read anything more complicated than "Come here, Jane." And even if she got past that, who would support her when she was in school? Not her parents, that's for sure! Half the time they didn't have the money to put a decent meal on the table. Her father was too busy carrying his cash to the track in the hopes of striking it rich, and her mother had a stack of lottery tickets running into a bundle of dollars that she spent in pursuit of the same hopeless fantasy.

School? Forget it, Rita had told the priest. She was as removed from that as her parents were, and at least she had the sense to know it. The best she could ever do would be to marry some guy. Maybe a guy who liked her looks, or something. That's why she had to get rid of the kid. Guys don't want to look at another man's brat all day. No, it was too bad, she said to herself, instinctively patting her swollen belly, but the kid had to go. *Had* to. But why did thinking about it make her cry?

The knock on the door was tentative. Rita wiped her eyes, then went to open it cautiously. Who would be standing on the other side of it? What would she be like? What was a person like who went shopping for a real live baby—her baby, Eddie's baby? Would she really be able to give the kid a better life? Would she really love the kid, or was it just going from poverty of money to poverty of love? The rage was coming up in her again and she tried to take a few breaths to control it. Well, maybe she *had* to sell the kid, she thought, but that didn't mean she had to be happy about it.

"Miss Briggs?" asked Sue Ellen, smiling widely under frightened eyes.

Miss Briggs, Rita thought bitterly. She hadn't been called Miss Briggs since the beauty contest when a judge asked her the question that lost her the contest: "What is your most cherished value, Miss Briggs?"

She had blanked completely. What a stupid question anyway! What was she supposed to say, her family? Her grandmother's antique doll? The answer that leaped to her mind was the only truthful one—winning! She had felt like screaming, "Winning, you dummy!" to the judge, but instead she searched her mind for an answer that would make her seem like a regular little cornfed American girl. But her mind had come up blank. Finally, she had muttered, "The freedom to ride in an automobile." The disappointed look in the judge's eyes told her everything she didn't want to know.

"Call me Rita," she corrected the brunette.

"May I come in, Rita?" Sue Ellen asked politely, like a five-year-old on the first day of school.

"Yeah. Why not?" was the sullen reply. The last thing she wanted was a stranger noseying through her place, but she supposed the woman had a right. If only she would wipe the dumb smile off her face. That would make it so much easier. If Sue Ellen had said, "I'm here to buy your baby. How much do you want?'' she might have liked her a lot more. But instead she seemed like one of those terminally nice people. People who had microwaves and new cars and good manners to boot. Those people made Rita sick.

Looking at her tiny room through Sue Ellen's eyes, Rita cringed. Since she rented the place she really hadn't done anything to try to make it look even a little better. Even her mother, no matter how low the dump they were living in, would put curtains on the windows and a little doily or something on the table.

But this place lacked even the basic amenities. Instead of curtains, she had put newspapers over the rods to keep out the prying eyes of her neighbors. The eating utensils were all made of plastic, mostly a dark red plastic with white chalky gouges in them.

Well, at least, the girl thought, the place didn't smell too bad. Rita had doused it with a bottle of pine cleaner because she hadn't been able to take the smell when she first walked in. The only bad smell would be in the toilet if the woman lifted the lid. But judging by the horrified look on her face as she surveyed the room, the woman wouldn't be using the bathroom.

"Want a root beer?" Rita asked.

"No, thank you," was the sincere and gentle reply.

Well, well, Rita thought, finally something was going right. "That's good. I only had one left and I want it myself."

Desperately seeking some charm in the situation, Sue Ellen decided that Rita's frank reply was amusing and she laughed lightly as if the girl had just made a witty comment. She was trying hard to like Rita. It meant a lot to her. After all, the memory of meeting her was something that time would never erase, no matter how old her son or daughter would become. It was a memory Sue Ellen would have to live with for the rest of her life. Even when Baby Ewing was grown and graduating from the best college in the country, she would remember this day, this woman, and this room.

"I don't see what's so funny about that," Rita said sulkily, moving to a pint-sized refrigerator that buzzed loudly when she opened the door.

The canned soda in her hand was like a weapon as Rita sat down on the dirty sofa and regarded Sue Ellen who stood politely, her Gucci handbag under her arm. "Sit down. Why're you standing? Sit down, will ya?" she snapped as if issuing an order.

"So," she continued as Sue Ellen gingerly sat down in a worn out wicker chair, "you're real rich, right?"

Rita's blue eyes were accusatory and bold. Sue Ellen seemed to shrink under their gaze. What could she say? She couldn't lie. And no matter how much she'd like to say, "Yes, but I wasn't born rich. I was born poor, too, just like you but I got out of it," she couldn't. None of her history mattered now. She *was* wealthy. That was the beginning and the end of it as far as the two women were concerned.

"Yes. I am wealthy," Sue Ellen answered gently.

"So what the hell's your problem? You got something wrong with you or something?"

"No," said Sue Ellen.

"Your husband got something wrong with him? What is it with you two?"

"No. There's nothing really wrong, except that my husband may have . . . um . . . well, he may have a problem with his . . . um . . . well, his organs or his hormones or something. We're not really sure."

Sue Ellen was smiling so broadly that her face hurt. J.R. would die if he knew she were in this room, talking to this girl, this unappealing girl who was going to be the real mother of his child. Her heart began beating wildly. The thought of J.R. discovering her sent panic shooting through her body. She had to remind herself that he had no reason to think she was up to anything and that her actions had been completely secret so far.

"Why don't you lose him? Get yourself a real man for a change," Rita was saying loftily, her feet crossed on the sofa.

A "real man." Was that the very phrase she had thrown at J.R. not a week before? Wasn't that the phrase that had driven him away from her in the dead of night? No wonder. It sounded so vulgar. Rita Briggs was as crude sober as Sue Ellen was when she was drunk. But Sue Ellen didn't blame the girl. And what could she say in response? She leaned back in the chair as it creaked in protest. She was lost, her feelings at sea. Maybe this wasn't a good idea after all.

"Oh, I get it. You don't want to lose out on his bucks."

Was that the real reason why she stayed with J.R., Sue Ellen wondered briefly? It couldn't be. It was so crude a reason and she told herself it wasn't true. She loved J.R., really and truly loved him. The fact that their marriage hadn't worked out didn't stand in

the way of that love. And though it was true that
there was a certain consolation in being "Mrs. J.R.
Ewing," well, what was wrong with that? Why
shouldn't she enjoy the privileges of the prestigious
name? Why shouldn't she enjoy the wealth she'd
married into? Hadn't she paid for it more dearly
than anyone could imagine? Maybe that's why she
did stay . . . but there was nothing wrong with that
as long as she was trying to make her marriage work.
That's what she had to focus on. That's why she
was here with this unfortunate pregnant girl.

Rita interrupted Sue Ellen's thoughts.

"Um . . . would you happen to have a cigarette? I
had a pack, but they ran out and I didn't have a
chance to get more 'cause I knew you were
coming."

Sue Ellen tried not to register her disapproval on
her face. Instead she tactfully said, "I'm sorry, Rita.
I don't smoke."

An uncomfortable silence settled over the room
until Sue Ellen drew up the courage to continue.
"And maybe you shouldn't either. When a pregnant
woman smokes, her baby's development is hurt
rather badly. Perhaps you didn't know that."

Rita didn't hesitate in her retort. "Look lady,"
she said in a tough, no-nonsense tone, "This baby
ain't your baby till it's out of my body and your
check has cleared the bank. So don't get righteous
on me, okay? It's none of your goddammed
business if I smoke or not!"

What more could be said? Rita's vitriolic outburst
had poisoned the proceedings for Sue Ellen.
*Everything was wrong with this girl! Everything was
wrong with the whole arrangement!*

Sue Ellen stood up to go. She still wanted to go through with an adoption, but there had to be a better way. Clearly this young woman hated herself, her baby and Sue Ellen.

"Where the hell are you going?" Rita asked incredulously.

"Well, perhaps you'd rather not have your privacy disturbed," Sue Ellen answered in a kind and sincere tone. "I can understand that."

Rita blocked her way, the seventh month of pregnancy between her and Sue Ellen. For the first time since Sue Ellen arrived, the girl smiled. "Sit down, will ya? Stop making a federal case out of everything." If Sue Ellen left there might not be another rich lady to bail her out of her problems. No, she would just convince Sue Ellen that her brusque manner was merely a part of her personality—a harmless part.

"I didn't mean to yell at you. I'm just a little flaky that way."

Sue Ellen sat again with relief.

"I only wish that we could be friends, Rita. I think that would make everything much more pleasant."

In a flash Rita lost whatever little control she had struggled to get. "Friends? What are you, a sicko or something? Why do you think I'm giving my baby away? 'Cause I want to? This baby is the last piece of my boyfriend and all I got in the world! If I had half a brain in my head I'd go back home, crawling all the way and beg my folks to take me back! You think they wouldn't? They'd be thrilled to have a grandkid! In fact, maybe I'll do just that! You rich think you can walk in here and tell me how to live my life! Well, you can get the hell out of here, okay?

I don't need you and I don't need your lousy money. My kid don't need you either!"

Sue Ellen had her hand on the doorknob. Why did everything she touched turn so sour? Here she had been unable even to have a civil talk with this poor and unfortunate young lady. If her own life had gone just a little differently, she might have been in the same circumstances.

"Rita," she said with a plea in her voice, "if you need anything, I'd be happy to help in any way."

If she needed anything, Rita thought? Sure she needed things. She needed lots of things. More than Sue Ellen could imagine.

"I don't need nothing from you, thank you," the girl answered bitterly.

"Not even some groceries? Some more root beer?" Sue Ellen asked, her voice trembling.

Oh, what the hell, Rita thought, sorry for her outburst. Nobody else was offering to do anything good for her.

"And maybe I could find you another apartment. This place doesn't have much room and it's kind of dark. Maybe a more cheerful place would make this an easier time for you."

Rita looked at Sue Ellen with bewilderment. What was this woman's guilt trip all about? Not that that was important. What *was* important was to get what you could while the getting was good. And this dame was willing to fork over money. If you had to sell your kid for it, well, that was just the way things were in real life.

"Sure. Get me an apartment. But someplace nice. The kind of place you'd live in. I want something really good, okay? And I better get it, 'cause you're getting the only thing I have in the world to give!"

With that, Sue Ellen smiled. Maybe everything would turn out fine after all. Soon, this would all be behind her and she would have a little child all her own to love.

"I'll get you something very special, Rita. Don't you worry."

"Okay," said the girl, her head hung down. "Listen, I gotta go to welfare."

"Fine, I have to leave, too," said Sue Ellen opening the door. "I'll see to it that you can move by this weekend."

After Rita closed the door softly behind Sue Ellen she put her hands on her belly. The baby kicked. Despite herself, Rita Briggs broke out in a flood of heartbroken tears.

Jock sat sunning himself on the mansion porch, a pitcher of cool lemonade at his side. He had been experiencing a real return of vigor—a thrilling feeling of energetic health that reminded him of the days when he was first building Ewing Oil and had had enough power in him to take on every supplier and buyer in the state of Texas. In those days he uncomplainingly put in fourteen-hour days. But now, and for the rest of his life, he would budget his energy more carefully. The future belonged to him and Ellie. There were cruises to take, new countries to travel to, dances to attend, and books to read together. Rocking himself now in the old wicker chair his mother-in-law first brought to Southfork, he felt a sense of a whole new life opening up for him. He would be an attentive husband and take his wife on a whirlwind of activity. They had both earned it, he thought, and besides, his affairs could be well taken care of by J.R. and Bobby.

Bobby strode across the lawn waving to his father. From the looks of the dirt on his denim jacket, Jock could tell Bobby had been hard at work on the ranch. He didn't find that thrilling but he could understand the attraction the land held for his son. Hadn't he felt the same pull to work with the earth that Bobby seemed to be feeling now? And however bad Jock felt about Bobby's absence from Ewing Oil, ranching sure beat the hell out of starting a construction company.

"Well, son—you look mighty tired," the older man said cheerfully, pouring Bobby a cool glass of lemonade. "Raoul forgot to put a little gin in there," he winked handing it to him. "But I suppose what we don't have won't harm us."

Bobby smiled and finished the tall glass in a moment.

"Good," was all he had to say.

"What's going on with Pamela, son? Want to talk about it?" Jock inquired, looking at his son intently.

"Nothing, Daddy," Bobby answered, amazed once again by his father's astute abilities to see into the hearts of the people around him.

"Now, come on, Bobby! You can't fool your daddy. Something is up. You two have been acting mighty serious around each other, and I can feel a tug of tension whenever you talk to each other."

It was true, Bobby thought. No matter how hard they were trying to stay friendly and light, the differences between them were beginning to take their toll on both of them. The ironic thing was that

Jock was partially the reason for their arguments lately. Bobby wanted his father to have a grandchild, *now*. He also found it hard to get past the notion that his father would be mighty disapproving if he heard about Pamela's new idea about getting herself a job. None of the Ewing women had ever worked—not since Jock had made his fortune—and the old man took that as something to be proud of.

"It's nothing, really, Daddy. Just a little argument. Nothing serious."

"Well, I don't want to butt in—but if you want to talk about it . . ."

Just then, Ellie appeared, carrying a bottle of pills and a glass of water for Jock.

"Morning, Mama," Bobby said warmly, kissing his mother on the cheek.

"Morning, Bobby. Looks as if you put in a hard day's work already, son. It's only eleven."

"We had a little problem with a steer, Mama. And now one of the irrigation pumps is acting up so I have to make a few phone calls."

"You and Pamela were awfully formal with each other this morning. No problem, I hope," Ellie remarked as she handed Jock his day's medication.

Jock and Bobby laughed. But his parents' comments made him wonder. How far were he and Pam being driven apart if the family could see it and he couldn't?

"Then she took off looking for you and when she got back she raced out of the driveway in your car looking as if she had to catch a train or something!" Ellie continued, her concern showing.

"Pam left?" Jock said alarmed. At first he had bitterly opposed Bobby's marriage to the Barnes girl, but in time, he had become fond of Pam. She was brighter than Sue Ellen and best of all, she made Bobby happy. Before he met Pam, Bobby had been troubled somehow. Maybe, he thought, it was all because of that Jenna Wade, Bobby's childhood sweetheart who had left him flat right before they were planning to get married. But for years after she left, Bobby had never been serious about another woman until Pam. Worse, he had drifted, never committing himself to any kind of work. Pam had brought out Bobby's ambition and Jock liked that.

"Nothing to be alarmed at, Daddy," Bobby was saying, "but, uh . . . well, Pam's decided to take her old job for a few months."

Bobby waited. That information had to be like a bomb to the members of the older generation, and yet they were oddly silent.

Suddenly, it happened. Jock stood up as if to leave the porch, his hands fluttering in front of him.

"I don't want to get upset," he said evenly. "I don't want to get upset, but—" Then it came, a loud Jock Ewing-style boom, like in the old days— "What the hell is that girl running off to a job for! She doesn't need the money, that's for sure! And Ewing women don't work! Didn't you tell her that, Bobby?"

Bobby was calm. Calmer than he had imagined he would be in this situation.

"Daddy, I don't think Pam sees herself as just a 'Ewing woman.' She has her own life to lead too."

Somehow, saying it, made him understand.

"What's wrong with being a Ewing woman!" Jock shouted. "It was good enough for your mother, wasn't it?"

"Well, Daddy, I just think Pam would like to have a little more to do with her life. The Daughters of the Alamo didn't really interest her," Bobby answered evenly, concealing the fear in his voice.

"Well, why can't she have a baby! She doesn't just have to sit around all day! If she wants to work, a baby will keep her plenty busy," Jock retorted forcefully.

Ellie stepped closer to her husband, putting her hands gently on his chest. "Jock, times have changed. A young girl today has a lot of opportunity that I never had. Now, there's nothing wrong with her taking a job. I probably would have taken one too if things had been different in our day. Bobby, I think you should be proud that Pam wants to work."

Jock looked at his wife in disbelief but decided the issue was not worth fighting about. His time in the hospital had taught him that nothing was more important than his health, and in order to guard that health he had to stay cool and calm when faced with problems. He sat down in the porch chair with a resigned look on his face.

Seeing his father behaving so meekly tore Bobby's heart. More than anything at that moment, he wanted to comfort Jock.

"Daddy, we'll have a baby. It's something we both want very much. But we're just not ready *now*. A baby would tie us down, and we'd like to have a year or two to enjoy each other and our freedom."

He was practically quoting Pam word for word, but now, saying it himself, he could perceive the wisdom of her outlook.

Jock sat silently for a minute, shaking his head in mild disgust. "Are you telling me that you honestly approve of your wife working?" Jock asked incredulously.

Bobby considered the question before he answered. "I'm not thrilled with it, Daddy, but I'm willing to make the adjustment."

Jock sighed. "Well, at least you're not still courting that crazy idea of starting a construction company."

Bobby considered telling his father the truth, but looking at Jock, Bobby saw how hard he was struggling to remain calm. It wouldn't be fair to upset him further, so Bobby said nothing.

Chapter Ten

Sue Ellen sat in the kitchen lingering over a cup of coffee she had made for herself. It was bitter. It had been a long time since she had faced the simple task of measuring and pouring even something as simple as her morning coffee for herself. For the past seven years, every meal she had eaten and every beverage she had drunk had been handed to her by the efficient servants Miss Ellie hired to look after the family's needs. Even nutritious snacks were available throughout the day for the Ewing family's pleasure.

But, today, Sue Ellen felt like "Sue Ellen Shepard," her maiden name before she had married J.R. and became a Ewing. Now that name was like a golden weight around her neck. She needed desperately to be alone to try to sort out some of her feelings. She had tried sitting in her bedroom in the morning, but images of J.R. kept crowding her there. So she had found her way to the kitchen where preparing and lingering over a cup of coffee were the props she needed for justifying her presence there.

Now that she would soon be a mother, sorting out her problems by drinking alcohol was out of the question. And as much as she would have liked to pour herself a good stiff drink now, she wouldn't. There was a baby involved here, and a husband, and a family. There was no one to talk to so she *had* to be her own best council—and that meant staying sober.

As she sat on the restored oak chair that had once been in Great Grandmother Southworth's old farmhouse outside Braddock, Sue Ellen saw Rita's face as it looked when she had first opened the door of her hovel of a rented room. It was a moment that was burned into Sue Ellen's memory. Meeting Rita Briggs had been fateful, and Sue Ellen could feel in her bones that her life was in for awesome transformation because of that meeting.

The situation played over and over like a movie in her mind, a movie in which the casting alone was perfect. Rita had J.R.'s coloring—the same brown hair and blue eyes. Even her facial structure matched J.R.'s—the nose especially, and large jaw. If Sue Ellen brought home a baby like Rita's, how could her husband possibly reject it? It would be tiny and helpless and theirs. And when he saw what a good mother Sue Ellen was, wouldn't he respect her for having had the gumption to get the baby? Wouldn't he admire the strength of her decision— and thank her for providing them with a beautiful little child they could call their own?

As sun streamed in through the windows facing the back gardens, Sue Ellen smiled to herself imagining the moment when she would place her baby in her husband's arms. She saw herself handing a warm bundle with a living, cooing baby to J.R. But then, a cold shiver ran through her as she fantasized seeing J.R.'s horrified face. What if he refused to accept the baby?

Sue Ellen shuddered as she remembered the discussions they had had in the past about adoption. He was totally and completely against the idea of adopting. He said it was something he refused even to consider. And no matter how hard Sue Ellen had pressed him for a logical reason for why he was so against it, all he ever had to say was that he didn't want to raise a baby that wasn't his own flesh and blood.

Her father-in-law felt the same way, too, He had made his ideas clear many times over the years. Whenever any acquaintance of the Ewings adopted a child, Jock would shake his head and cluck as if he couldn't understand how people could do something so foolish. And to back up his prejudice, he had a whole repertoire of stories about adopted children who were ungrateful to their adopted parents. He told these stories with righteous vigor as if ungrateful *natural* children never existed.

Shaking her head lightly, Sue Ellen couldn't avoid asking herself how she could really think that Jock and J.R.'s strong feelings would ever change. What if she brought her helpless little baby into the house and the two of them viciously threw her and the baby out? They had the meanness in them to do it. Hadn't they gotten rid of Gary and his wife once?

For a moment Sue Ellen was paralyzed with the feeling that there was no way she could bring home an adopted baby—no matter how much that baby resembled J.R. She tried to face the possibility maturely, but despite herself, tears formed in her eyes. The thought of losing Rita's baby was devastating. And if she didn't adopt, what other choice did she have? J.R. refused to see a fertility specialist and he hardly ever made love with her any more.

Suddenly a surge of strength ran through Sue Ellen. She had vowed to be her own woman and act on her own behalf and she owed it to herself to follow through. If she was going to get a baby, adoption was the only way. And then if J.R. refused to accept the baby, she would take it and move far away from Southfork and the Ewings and even, Dallas. In the end, she thought fearfully, she wanted a baby that much. She could take the child to Boca Raton, Florida, where her mother lived. Her mother wouldn't like it, but she wouldn't refuse to take her daughter and grandchild in until Sue Ellen got settled. Maybe, in time, she'd meet another man—a warm, kind man, a man who truly and honestly loved her—

But in her heart, she knew it would never come to that. J.R. would never let her go any more than he would throw away a pair of expensive gold cuff links. Sue Ellen was a valuable asset to him, well-spoken and attractive. Their marriage was something he was proud of and he made a great show of having it appear like a "perfect marriage" to the rest of the world. Admitting failure as a husband in front of his family was something he would never do. There had never been a divorce in the Ewing family, and J.R. would not be able to take the embarrassment of having the first one.

So, she thought, clinging to rationality and pushing her tears away, he was sure to accept Rita's baby—or would he? Sue Ellen's thinking had just come around the same terrible circle, and she hung her head in despair.

At that moment, Miss Ellie walked into the kitchen from the mansion porch. She was bringing fresh tomatoes she'd picked from her garden to add to the supper Teresa would prepare later that night. No matter how wealthy she might ever be, the taste of her own homegrown fruits and vegetables was one of her grandest pleasures. These ripe and luscious tomatoes beat the store-bought kind any day, she knew, and were worth the time and effort it took to cultivate them. Ellie smiled as she placed the basket on the shelf by the entrance. It was as if the sun had followed her inside, clinging to her face and clothes even after she had stepped into the indoor light.

It was a surprise for her to see Sue Ellen sitting at the table all alone. She knew the family, especially the younger members, seldom used the kitchen at Southfork. The Southfork kitchen just wasn't the kind of place her mother's kitchen had been where farmers and their neighbors, young and old, congregated to laugh and talk and cry when they had to. This kitchen was more a place where the servants worked. Only when a family member wanted to be alone would they even think of going there. Ellie could tell right away that something was wrong.

Her daughter-in-law looked small and forlorn as she sat bent over a cup of cold coffee. What had J.R.

done now, Ellie thought with exasperation?

"Why, Sue Ellen—what a surprise to find you here."

"Oh, Miss Ellie, hello."

Sue Ellen looked longingly at her mother-in-law, then turned her eyes away before she thought Ellie would see the need in them.

"Is something the matter, Sue Ellen? You look a little sad."

Ellie didn't usually like to share her observations of people, but Sue Ellen seemed to be holding some kind of heavy burden inside. Sometimes, giving people an opening helped them to express the troubling thoughts that were defeating them.

Sue Ellen again looked at her mother-in-law. Miss Ellie was so wise and so understanding—the very opposite of J.R., she thought bitterly. How could *this* mother have ever produced a son like J.R.? But if she knew what Sue Ellen was planning to do, would she understand?

If only she could broach the subject with her mother-in-law. Perhaps Miss Ellie would be able to shed some light on the whole complicated and emotional situation, Sue Ellen thought. She had to try. She had to. She had kept the adoption a secret all this time, but now the time was coming when the secret would have to be revealed. Rita Briggs would soon enter her eighth month of pregnancy and Sue Ellen could be getting a call from the doctors any day after that.

Sue Ellen decided to take the plunge. She *had* to talk to someone—if she didn't, she thought she would go mad.

"Oh, Miss Ellie—I've just been so troubled about

this baby thing," she began awkwardly. "You know I want a baby so very much and J.R. and I have tried and tried . . . but nothing ever seems to happen. J.R. says I shouldn't worry about it, but it's been almost eight years and—it's gotten to the point that—well, I know J.R. and Jock don't usually approve of this kind of thing but, there are so many unwanted children in the world—and I thought— maybe we should just go ahead and . . ."

Sue Ellen was about to say, "adopt," but the word stuck in her throat and her voice trailed off to silence. Ellie stood still listening seriously to Sue Ellen, her face unreadable. Looking at it, Sue Ellen thought that everything was going wrong. How could she have expected support and understanding from Miss Ellie—she was Jock's wife after all. Now, having practically told her mother-in-law about her plan, she put her head down in shame. She didn't want to see Miss Ellie's scowl of disapproval.

Ellie took a long hard look at her troubled daughter-in-law. Poor Sue Ellen, she thought, she's as fragile as a lily and she's lost, so lost. Ellie knew J.R. was not an easy man to live with and it was plain to see that Sue Ellen wasn't having an easy time of it. Maybe a baby would bring them closer together. J.R. often surprised people by his kindness toward children. Maybe having a child of his own would help soften his personality and make him a kinder and more loving person. But if they were hoping to conceive after seven years of infertility they were way off the track. It was time for J.R. and his wife to face the facts.

"You know, Sue Ellen, I think adoption is a wonderful way to have a child. My cousin Florence adopted her son, Ashley, many years ago and the two of them are as close as I am to my boys. If I were you I would seriously consider adoption. You'll find, dear, that being a mother is all about the care you give a child and the love. Birth stops after a few hours, but motherhood lasts a lifetime. And I have the feeling that having a baby around might be a very good thing for J.R."

Had she heard right, Sue Ellen wondered, her heart beating fast as her lethargy lifted? Miss Ellie was sanctioning everything she'd been planning and working on! How Sue Ellen longed to tell her mother-in-law about Rita Briggs and the baby that would be born in just a couple of short months! But sharing that news could still be dangerous. J.R. might somehow find out and that could change everything. He couldn't know yet. He had to find out only after the baby was born and was safe at home. Besides, if Miss Ellie was the only one to support her, she could still be in for a hard time with Jock and J.R.

Sue Ellen decided to play her cards carefully, but to bring up the obstacle that was still facing her.

"But I don't know how Jock or J.R. would take to the idea of having an adopted baby in this family, Miss Ellie. I once heard them talking about it and they didn't seem very favorable."

"Now, Sue Ellen," was Miss Ellie's gentle advice, "don't you worry about Jock! I can take care of him. He may *think* he's opposed to having an adopted grandchild, but I know him. Once he holds his own little grandchild in his arms, he'll consider that child to be one hundred percent *Ewing*! I'll personally vouch for that!"

Sue Ellen looked up at her mother-in-law. If she cried with relief and gratitude, would Miss Ellie suspect she had taken any action? She couldn't take the chance, so she turned her head away as tears of relief came to her eyes.

"You take care of J.R., Sue Ellen," the older woman went on. "If a baby would be good for your marriage, then you've got to do whatever you can."

Sue Ellen could hold her gratitude in no longer. At last there was one person in this world who understood.

Rising from the table she went to her mother-in-law and kissed her, then buried her face in her shoulder.

"Thank you for your support, Miss Ellie. It means more to me than you will ever know."

When Lucy saw Ray Krebbs crossing the lawn from the corral to the stables she ran up to him playfully.

"Ray! Just the man I was looking for! Come on! Put on your trunks and we can swim!"

The usually friendly foreman simply shook his head negatively. "Not today. Too much work, Lucy," he said to the girl who stood before him wearing a tiny red bikini.

Lucy and Ray had always had a special friendship. Maybe it was because the girl felt fatherless, but she had a special fondness for the rancher who was so down-to-earth and who knew so much about nature. When Lucy was just a little girl, Ray would let her watch the new foals after they'd been born and he'd let her stand in the back of the pickup truck when he had to make a tour of the ranch. Their friendship was strong, long-standing, uncomplicated and innocent.

However, now that Lucy was growing up, Ray wanted to make sure it stayed that way. Sometimes it was almost as if Lucy were flirting with him. Today, for instance, he was aware of an undeniable gleam in her eye when she invited him for a swim, and he wasn't having any of it. He knew Lucy was going through a rebellious time and he didn't want to be around when the fallout came. And you can't be too careful around a Ewing woman, he reasoned to himself.

"Oh, don't be an old fuddy-duddy! Grampa's at the doctor's, Bobby's in town and J.R. is upstairs! Live a little! All work and no play make Ray a dull boy, you know!"

Just then, J.R. strode from the house where he had been looking for Sue Ellen. He had decided to take the day off from work—something he did occasionally when things at the office were running exceptionally smoothly. Taking a day off when he wanted was a privilege that the president of the company could take, and J.R. liked to exercise that privilege.

Ever since Bobby's exit, life at Ewing Oil had been as smooth as glass for J.R. He felt a vigor and enthusiasm for life that he hadn't felt in all the months Bobby was interfering with his running of the company. But now, J.R.'s life was proceeding perfectly. He was feeling so good in fact that he had decided to surprise his wife by taking her out to lunch. Laurie's girl had had a talk with him about Sue Ellen, and he realized he had been neglecting his wife a little too much recently. And since she had apparently stopped drinking at his strong request, it might be the perfect time to give her a little treat as a reward.

Watching Lucy talk to Ray, J.R. made a mental note that the time had come to break up that friendship. Lucy didn't seem to realize how womanly her body had become over the past year or two and the effect that a red string bikini would have on any man.

"Ray!" he called in an authoritative voice. "Don't you have some work to do on that irrigation well?" It paid to keep up with what was happening on the ranch, J.R. thought.

"Yes, J.R.," was Ray's reply.

"Then why don't you get to it instead of talking to my niece. She'll keep you all day with that silly chitchat of hers and the whole ranch will go to seed."

"Sure enough," Ray replied. "See ya, Lucy," he said before he marched off to the irrigation area.

Lucy sighed. It was lonely on the ranch.

"Don't you think it would be a good idea to start wearing some clothes now that your body is popping out all over the place?" J.R. asked Lucy tactlessly.

But his niece brazenly stood before him and answered, "I wanted to get a tan. Do you want me to wear a ski suit or something?"

As she spoke, Lucy was aware of the truth of his words. Her body *had* developed—and her figure was much fuller than she'd ever dreamed it would be. She had to admit she was pretty pleased with the way she looked in this bathing suit. She was not at all concerned about J.R.'s opinion.

Well, tough, she thought. J.R. liked to control everything, but he couldn't control her choice of clothes. She was proud of the body God gave her and she had no intention of hiding it away under some prim school-girl outfit just to please J.R. Ewing!

"Where's Sue Ellen?" he asked, tired already of Lucy's company.

"How should I know?" was his niece's tart reply. "She's *your* wife, not mine," she added coldly.

"That's funny. I thought she'd be here," J.R. muttered, more to himself than to Lucy. But the girl couldn't miss an opportunity to upset her uncle.

"I haven't seen her in weeks, Uncle dear. She's hardly *ever* home any more. Even when you're at work, she takes off in the morning, stays out all day, and hurries home right before you get here."

"Well, Lucy," J.R. replied, a bit softer than usual, "she's got that Library benefit coming up and she's busy with that. She's the head of the committee, you know."

Lucy was surprised that J.R. knew so much about his wife. Maybe he really did care under that old exterior. If so, what she was about to say was even more delicious.

"Really, J.R.?" she said with as much urbane sophistication as she could muster, "I think it has more to do with that man she's seeing. You know, the lawyer."

"Oh?" was his casual-sounding reply.

"Yes. I guess they're just . . . well, close friends, 'cause he calls here all the time—and she's always running into town at a moment's notice to see him."

J.R. had no intention of biting—he knew how much Lucy hated him—and the feeling was decidedly mutual. The thought of having to share a sizable inheritance with this no-account brat someday was extremely disturbing to him. But there was little he could do to get rid of Lucy now. Until she was fully grown, he had to put up with her presence at Southfork.

"I'm sure it's nothing Lucy. Don't you worry your pretty little head about me and Sue Ellen."

Lucy was prepared for the rebuff. She acted as if he hadn't said a word as she added, "And then there's her new apartment. I'm sure it takes a lot of time decorating."

"Okay, Lucy. What are you saying now?" J.R. looked at his niece with narrow eyes.

"Oh, nothing really," was the girl's flip reply. "Just that someone called here about a cleaning contract on an apartment that Mrs. Ewing, Sue Ellen Ewing, had taken in downtown Dallas. That's all. Just a little *pied-à-terre* on Worthington Street. I guess," she added, saucily, "that's where she and her friend go to—ahem, work on that library benefit."

"What was this fellow's name did you say?" J.R. asked, his eyes like steel.

"Didn't say, Uncle. But it's Buzz Conners. And he sounds very cute on the phone, too."

J.R. had nothing more to say to his niece. Glaring at her, he turned on his heel and walked back into the house.

Sue Ellen was unused to the feel of jeans. Every season when she bought her wardrobe she always bought a couple of pairs out of habit, but she usually kept them in the back of her closet with the labels still on them until they were given to charity the next time the opportunity arose.

It was mostly because J.R. didn't like his wife to wear jeans; he felt they were unbecoming on a lady—"dungarees," he called them, with the emphasis on the first syllable. They were suitable for ranch hands but not for women. One of his petty annoyances with Lucy and his sister-in-law was that, unlike Sue Ellen who at least dressed tastefully, they often appeared around Southfork in blue jeans. In matters of dress Sue Ellen liked to please him. It was a small aspect of their relationship but one that was trouble free and so Sue Ellen cherished it. But today, jeans were necessary. Today, she was helping someone move.

Her hair pulled back and tucked under a kerchief, Sue Ellen felt a little like a college girl. She had called professional movers to take most of Rita's goods, but since the girl wasn't ready when the van arrived, Sue Ellen found herself toting cartons of pots and pans from the trunk of her Mercedes.

Rita's new apartment building was tall and white, only ten years old. The apartment faced south and west, so a stream of light flooded the rooms all day. But no matter how hot it might be, Rita would be comfortable. The quiet whirring of the air conditioning system took care of the inhabitants' comfort at all times.

"So, what do you think?" Sue Ellen anxiously asked the girl who was walking from room to room taking in her new living space. The apartment was stunning. It was bright, airy, and tastefully furnished with batik and rattan in pastel colors. The apartment made Rita feel like a film star or an heiress. Just walking through the rooms and knowing that the place was hers gave her an unbelievable thrill. But letting Sue Ellen know how she felt could be dangerous.

Looking at the wealthy woman, Rita shrugged unenthusiastically. She had Sue Ellen all figured out. She had known a lot of Sue Ellens—they were the masochists of the world, always looking for approval from others, always doubting themselves and feeling guilty for no good reason. And the guiltier they felt the easier it was to deal with them—and the more they came across with.

"It's all right," she said noncomittally as Sue Ellen reached inside yet another box to empty it. "The bedroom's kinda small," she added critically, although the bedroom of the apartment was twice the size of her last room.

Sue Ellen was hurt, but she continued unpacking. Reaching into a liquor store carton, she pulled out a framed 8"x10" glossy photograph of a young woman at a beauty contest. Looking at it more closely, she realized that the beautiful girl in the picture was Rita. The picture appeared to be taken at some kind of podium. Rita was standing next to it, smiling at the man beside her who was handing her a large bouquet of red roses. She was dressed in what appeared to be a frothy prom dress and she wore a banner that read "Miss Teen Sweetwater."

The face looked basically the same as Rita's did now as she stood looking out the windows of her new apartment onto the church steeple below. But the body was slender and lithesome despite the girl's full bosom. Staring at the photo, Sue Ellen saw Rita as a radiant beauty as she smiled happily into the camera's lens while reaching for the flowers.

"Oh, my goodness!" she exclaimed. "You look beautiful in this picture! Very beautiful!" The compliment was entirely sincere. The photo of Rita projected an innocent sweetness that anyone would find beautiful.

For a moment Rita looked shocked, then she yelled, "Hey! Leave my things alone, will ya! That's not yours!" and snapped the photo angrily from Sue Ellen's hands. But there was a hint of vulnerability on Rita's face as she looked at the picture herself— something Sue Ellen hadn't seen before.

"Why, Rita! You won a beauty contest? That's wonderful!"

"Miss Teen Sweetwater. Big deal," was the sour reply. "When I got to Miss Teen Texas I lost."

"I was in a beauty pageant once," Sue Ellen said, happy at last to have something in common with the girl who would be her child's biological mother.

"Oh, yeah?" Rita asked with more interest than hostility for a change. "Which one?"

"Miss Texas."

"How'd you do?"

"Well—" Sue Ellen suddenly regretted bringing up the pageant. "I, uh, I was crowned Miss Texas that year. It was a long time ago," she added, in hopes of minimizing her winning experience.

The girl's friendliness withered as she shook her head in disgust. "You rich dames always get whatever you want. It's sickening."

"Well," said Sue Ellen patiently and apologetically, "I didn't get Miss America. And I really wanted that. I didn't even make the finals. It was the first time in ten years that a Miss Texas didn't make the finals. It was horrible."

Rita was looking at Sue Ellen almost with compassion. "Did you cry?" she asked sincerely.

"Yes. I did. For three days straight," was the honest reply.

"I cried when I lost Miss Teen Texas, too."

The two women were silent. Then, Rita smiled at Sue Ellen. It was a sad smile, but a genuine one. I understand, the smile seemed to say. In that moment, there was a perceptible change in their feelings toward one another. Sue Ellen, who had longed for Rita's acceptance, felt that she finally had it. She could be more secure now.

As for Rita, she was beginning to see Sue Ellen as simply another human being—not an emissary from the faraway and unattainable world of wealth, but a real woman, made of flesh and blood. The wall between them was beginning to crumble.

Chapter Eleven

Liz Craig, impeccably dressed but for the pencil tucked behind her ear, laughed with delight behind the tall glass partition bordering the display racks of The Store. Pamela Barnes Ewing was back on staff at last, and The Store finally had a buyer who knew what she was doing. Already Pamela had ordered a bunch of Japanese sweatshirts with hand-painted pictures of automobiles and airplanes, and now the shirts were flying off the racks at $50 apiece. Watching yet three more customers select them, she shook her head in happy disbelief. Only Pamela would have seen the sales potential of those shirts. To Liz they looked like items better suited to the The Store's Boy's department.

"I've got to hand it to you, sister, you have the magic touch!" she said to Pamela who was drinking tea from a Styrofoam cup on her well-earned break. "Those shirts seemed *tres* fifth grade to me when I saw them coming in. But watching them leave the place is *magnifique*!"

"Thanks, Liz. In fact, I think I'll take one for my niece Lucy," Pam said, her feet elevated on the folding chair in front of her. "They're just about her speed."

"Well, forget the store discount. Take it as a gift from me as manager, okay?" Liz told her.

Just then the white phone on the wall behind Liz rang and the manager picked it up. Pamela relaxed as Liz nodded into the phone. "All right. All right. All right! I'll tell her," she laughed, hanging up with a dramatic flourish.

"Your brother is certainly an insistent guy. He wants to know why you're late for lunch and to tell you to get the hell over to the restaurant!"

"Oh, my God! Cliff! I forgot all about him!"

Pamela scrambled to her feet and reached for her lavender jacket on the wall. "I'm gone—but, oh, Liz! If Bobby calls, tell him I'll call him back, okay?" Pam hadn't yet given up hope that her husband would think things through and put through a call apologizing for his cold behavior to her that morning. Ever since she had actually started back to work at The Store, he had been cold and grumpy to her in the mornings.

Taking the time to call to apologize was something they both did when things weren't right between them. This time, Pam was so eager for them to have good feelings again that she almost considered calling *him* to apologize. But what for, she had to ask herself calmly and rationally? She hadn't done anything wrong, She certainly had a right to her own life, after all!

Hurrying through the crowds of fashionably dressed shoppers, Pam decided to leave the shop by the side entrance. That meant rushing through the men's department, which was usually not so crowded in the middle of the day, and the infant's department, which was never crowded.

She saw them from across the room. Sue Ellen was with a pasty-faced pregnant teenager who was holding up a bunting set for Sue Ellen's apparent approval. On her sister-in-law's arm there were several infant outfits—one more expensive than the other. What was going on, Pam wondered?

"Sue Ellen!" she called.

Sue Ellen turned around, the color draining from her face. "Why, Pamela!" She walked a few steps away from Rita who might have been just another shopper looking at the colorful mobiles that were for hanging on the side of a crib. Seeing that Pam was glancing at the clothing on her arm, she explained quickly.

"My friend is having a baby and I've been invited to her shower."

Pam was surprised. In the year that she had known her sister-in-law, she had never seen Sue Ellen with a friend. The women in the Daughters of the Alamo were mostly past their childbearing years, and Sue Ellen had never once received a guest at Southfork or ever gone visiting any friends, to the best of Pam's knowledge. Still, she didn't want to seem impolite.

"Must be a very close friend. Those are beautiful things you've got there."

Just then, Rita popped out from behind a display case holding a mobile made of stuffed monkeys who sang, "Over the Rainbow" as they turned and danced.

"Mrs. Ewing, check this out!" the girl was practically shrieking like a baby herself in a store full of lollipops.

Sue Ellen winced with embarrassment but called out softly, "It's very cute. If you want it, we'll take it." Rita squealed with delight and then took off again.

"I'm . . . um . . . I'm doing a little charity work for the Daughters," Sue Ellen hurriedly fabricated. "That young lady is an unwed mother, and I thought I'd take her shopping for a few little things."

Two lies were one too many. She quickly added, "Especially since I was already shopping for my friend's shower."

Pamela looked at her sister-in-law trying hard to hide her disbelief.

"Well," she said, sounding as sincere as possible, "that's very nice of you, Sue Ellen. I'm sure she appreciates it very much."

Rita, out of curiosity, had positioned herself close enough to the Ewing women to hear what they said while remaining unseen. What she heard shocked her as she listened to Sue Ellen embellishing her lies to make them more believable, her voice soft and conspiratorial.

"She's a reformed drug addict from Rochester, New York, but she came to Dallas to have her baby so that no one in her family would know about it. Actually she's a niece of Martha Heinekker's—but don't breathe a word of it to Martha or even mention that you know she has a niece—the embarrassment would kill her."

Sue Ellen had taken her sister-in-law by the arm and was walking away from the infant's department.

"And Pam, please, don't mention this to J.R. or Bobby either, okay? You know, J.R. doesn't think I should do as much charity work as I do, and I'd rather this be our little secret."

Pam was incredulous. Did Sue Ellen really believe Pam would swallow any of this? And what was *really* going on?

"I won't mention it, Sue Ellen. And good luck. I have to go now, I'm meeting Cliff for lunch."

"Oh?" Sue Ellen said pleasantly. "Well, that's too bad. But please give your brother my warmest regards and do enjoy your lunch."

Sue Ellen's smile seemed to crack her face as she stood waving to Pamela until the other woman found the exit.

Then, turning to Rita in a flash, she grabbed the girl's arm lightly. "Let's get out of here, please, before I run into anybody else I know!"

It was always wise to keep a detective or two on your informal staff, J.R. thought proudly. That's why he paid Chuck Manson by the month whether he needed his services or not.

J.R. prided himself on being a polite person. Nothing annoyed him more than the so-called open and honest people of the world who felt they had to meet every crisis head on. In marriage, they were the people who felt you should have no secrets from your mate. In business, they were the people who liked everyone to keep their books open in order to assure a "fair deal" for everyone. If they caught a person stealing, they'd call him in for a talk. If they found their mate cheating, they'd go to them with the evidence and have it out, their pain falling

sloppily about them like mewling babies. Not J.R.
To him, a real man didn't confront. He acted, but
not crudely—not brashly, unless there were no other
options.

J.R. believed in the subtle effects of sabotage and
deceit. If Sue Ellen *was* cheating on him, she would
have a heavy price to pay. But he would find out first
and act later. And he was damned sure he wouldn't
find out by asking!

"Chuck?" he said into the phone after his
secretary had placed the call. "Say, I need your help
on a little matter."

The man at the other end of the line would be
only too happy to oblige. His association with the
well-known Mr. J.R. Ewing had provided him with a
virtual fountain of extra cash over the years. Thanks
to J.R.'s monetary supplements, Manson had been
able to do things like buy himself a sailboat, get his
wife a sewing machine and send his daughter to
Beauty School—without having to scrimp and save
for those things.

"Name it, Mr. Ewing, and I'm at your service."

That was just the response J.R. wanted to hear.
Manson was a man you could trust: he was
respectful and he knew his place.

"Great, Chuck. It involves a personal matter.
Could you do a little discreet checking on a Buzz
Connors? He might be a lawyer. I just want to know
a little bit about the man, his personal habits and so
forth."

J.R. leaned back in his leather chair as he spoke.
He closed his eyes just for a second as he gathered
himself, leaned forward and added, almost casually,
"You know my wife, Sue Ellen, don't you, Chuck?"

"Well, sir. I've never had the pleasure of meeting Mrs. Ewing personally, but I did see her many times last year when you requested that I check up on her."

"Right. Well, maybe you could find out what she's been up to these days. You might start looking on Worthington Street. I think she goes there every so often. Find out and get back to me right away on this, will you?

"Yes, sir," said the detective respectfully.

J.R. hung up the phone and swiveled his chair so that he could look out onto the city of Dallas. Last year he had suspected Sue Ellen of cheating, but Manson had found out she was clean. He didn't want to jump to any conclusions now. But it did worry him that she had made those sexual advances to him a few weeks ago. That kind of behavior was very unusual for Sue Ellen, and if she acted that way out of the house there was no telling the kind of response she might get. Sue Ellen really was a beautiful woman, J.R. thought, and if she got drunk enough she might do anything.

J.R. shook his head. He was worried. If she *was* cheating on him, he would have to come down hard on her. He would ruin the man, too. This Connors would have to leave the state of Texas, and he probably wouldn't leave it in one piece either. There were plenty of people willing to break a few bones for extra dollars—and J.R. had plenty to spend on a worthy cause. If Sue Ellen was cavorting with this Connors, he'd like to do the bone-breaking himself. Of course, that was just a fantasy. J.R. would never let his hands get dirty acting like a jealous husband for all the world to see. Doing the dirty work was a little pleasure he'd have to deny himself for the sake of propriety.

Infidelity was no reason for a divorce, either, he thought as he toyed unconsciously with the little brass oil derrick that served as a paperweight. There would be no public parting of the ways no matter what happened—not even if his worst suspicions were all true. At that point, divorce would be too good for Sue Ellen. No, he'd stay married to her all right, and she could shop to her heart's content, but he'd make certain, in his own genteel way, that she paid, and paid, and paid!

Cliff was eating a burger with his campaign manager when Pamela walked into the restaurant. Since they were engrossed in animated conversation, Pam merely nodded and took a seat until her brother was free.

"Well, check the south side! Rents can't be that high there! And there's got to be a storefront that's just sitting empty! Look, Charlie—we *need* a campaign office, and preferably one near the university," Cliff was saying.

"Yeah, the college kids all love you, Cliff. If we get an office near a university, we'll have plenty of volunteers. Anybody who's against the Ewings makes a big impression on those young minds, thank God! No offense, Pam," the man added.

Pam nodded, patiently, trying to project a modicum of civility. She had heard it all before—many times. And now she knew she'd have to hear it a lot more since Cliff was actually on the campaign trail working day and night to defeat the big oil industry that the Ewing name was synonymous with. To the extent that his political views were formed by his personal vendetta against Jock and J.R., she disapproved of his actions. But she had to admit, big oil had ignored most of the basic rules of environmental protection, and that had to change if the ecology of the state was to survive.

"Okay, get outta here! I've got a lunch date with my sister."

The campaign manager left as Cliff apologized to Pam.

"Sorry I already started lunch, Pam, but where the hell were you? You said you'd be here at noon! I even called the ranch looking for you. That's how I found out you were at The Store—your loving husband told me."

"Oh? How did he sound?" Pam wanted to know, her anxiety showing. For a minute, she felt like a teenager asking a friend what a boy said about her when she wasn't there.

"Not thrilled. He told me you were taking a job."

Pam smiled and nodded her head.

Cliff was amazed. "Why? Don't you get enough to eat out there at Southfork?"

"Come on, Cliff. Don't be like the Ewings! They're all against the idea of my working and I don't need you on the same side!"

"But, Pam, honey, get real!" Cliff said, forcefully. "You taking a job—well, it doesn't make any sense!"

"Cliff," Pam leaned in and put on a serious face, though her eyes betrayed an impish grin. "It's important to show the world that we Ewings have the common touch."

Cliff laughed. "And you're not the only Ewing

who's going after the common touch. Your sister-in-law is doing pretty well for herself in that direction, too!"

"What are you talking about?" Pam asked.

"Don't you know? Sue Ellen has been consulting with Buzz Connors. Now, you don't get more common than good old Buzz!"

"Come on, Cliff! Sue Ellen doesn't need the services of a Buzz Connors—she's got the best lawyers in Dallas available to her whenever she needs them!"

"Well, maybe the best lawyers couldn't help her, but Buzz could. It would depend on what she was doing. She's not trying to adopt a baby, is she? Buzz does a lot of those so-called private adoptions, the kind most lawyers won't touch."

"Cliff!" Pam said emphatically, "J.R. would never adopt a baby!"

"What can I tell you? I saw them together and she was signing some papers. What else could it be?"

What else indeed, Pam thought, thinking of Sue Ellen's embarrassed face when she ran into her at The Store. But there was no sense in jumping to any conclusions. The whole thing might have been completely innocent. Maybe Sue Ellen got a traffic ticket that she didn't want J.R. to know about—that could explain her going to a strange lawyer. But if she *was* adopting, Pam thought, did she really think she could get away with it?

As Sue Ellen and Rita loaded the packages in the back of the Mercedes, the pregnant woman was strangely quiet.

What could it be, now, Sue Ellen wondered, the

slightest bit of annoyance beginning to surface in her. She had just gotten herself a complete wardrobe and helped Sue Ellen shop for the baby in the most indulgent way possible. Even the saleswoman in the store had been flushed with delight as she tallied the bill. It had been astronomical! The baby not only had a complete layette, but snowsuits, swim suits, and even a tiny bathrobe. Rita had picked out mobiles, stuffed toys and music boxes, enough for ten babies, to complete the day's shopping.

Then it hit Sue Ellen—hard. It was only natural for Rita to be upset. All of these things were for the baby she would bear in great pain, only to hand it over to someone else. A twinge of compassion, guilt, and pity shot through Sue Ellen's body, but she quickly steeled herself and worked to reverse it, telling herself the die had already been cast. There was no way for either Rita or Sue Ellen to change their minds now. The papers had been signed. Besides, hadn't Rita initiated the sale when she found Buzz Connors? The arrangement had been completely voluntary, and if the girl was regretting the decision now that the birth came closer and closer—well, that was horrible, but it was just too bad.

Driving along the streets of Dallas, Sue Ellen had to bite her lip hard so that she would say nothing to Rita. Introducing the subject would be disastrous now that the reality was approaching.

The silence in the car was terribly loud as the two women rode back to the girl's apartment. And it was only when they were on the elevator to her apartment that Rita broke the horrible silence.

"I heard you talking to that lady, you know.

'Reformed drug addict.' Gimmee a break. What the hell is going on with you anyway?" she spit out to Sue Ellen.

Sue Ellen sighed with relief to know that Rita's problem only had to do with her pride and her ego.

"Oh, Rita, I'm so sorry," Sue Ellen said sincerely, "but that woman was my sister-in-law, and I couldn't take the chance that she would tell my family that I'm adopting a baby."

Rita looked at Sue Ellen with bewilderment and shock.

"What the hell are you talking about? You mean your family doesn't know about this? What about your husband? He knows, doesn't he?"

Sue Ellen couldn't lie. Though hearing the truth from someone else's voice made the whole situation sound terribly wrong.

"I couldn't tell him, Rita!" she pleaded. "Please try to understand. My husband is a terribly stubborn man and he doesn't approve of adoption. He would force me to give up the baby if he knew, and I can't take that chance. It means too much to me!"

Everything she was saying was the raw truth. And the depth of her despair about J.R. showed even to Rita. What kind of life would her baby have, the girl wondered? Would the child's new father reject it? Be mean to it?

Rita forced these thoughts out of her mind. None of it mattered. She wouldn't let it matter. The only important thing was getting the two thousand bucks and getting the hell out of Dallas.

It was after dinner, and light rain was falling quietly on the trees as Bobby lay face down on his big bed in agony. He had a pillow under his chin as Pam gently massaged and stroked the aching muscles in his back. The strong scent of wintergreen penetrated the room, which was brightened with a soft pink light.

"Arrrggghh" Bobby moaned in pain.

"Am I being too rough?" Pam asked, stopping the massage in an instant, but holding her hands on his back.

"No!" was the emphatic reply. "Keep going!"

"Well, that just sounded like it hurt."

"It did hurt! But it was a good hurt. Please, don't stop. You'll never know how much I need this, Pammy."

Pam smiled and began again.

"I guess sitting in an office wasn't the best preparation for wrestling with steers," she told her husband sympathetically as she continued massaging his wide, muscular shoulders.

"Well, at least ranching was my own idea— nobody else's. And it's funny, but I like it. It's the perfect thing for me to be doing right now. Right about six inches—up a little—ahhhh! There!—This is really going to get me in shape if it doesn't kill me. And I'm going to stick with it, too. At least till Daddy gets back on his feet. Then I'm going to begin looking into that construction idea I have. I should have plenty of strength and stamina for business by then! Ahhh . . . That's so good, Pammy. What would I ever do without you?"

"Don't worry about it. I'm not going anywhere," Pam said lightly.

"I know."

Pam continued stroking Bobby in silence,

connected by the feel of skin and warm hands.

"Honey, I'm so happy that you understand about the job and everything. That makes a big difference to me. I hated knowing you were feeling bad about it."

"Well, I just didn't understand until I talked with Daddy. He really set me straight about the whole thing."

"Your father? Now, that's funny. I would never in a million years have thought that Jock would understand why I wanted to go back to work. I guess I didn't give him enough credit."

Bobby chuckled softly, raising his body onto his elbow and rolling over, feeling relaxed and satisfied. Just looking at his smiling wife, he felt a warm glow.

"Well, it didn't exactly happen like that, honey," he said sheepishly. "What happened was that Daddy was so against the idea that he went into a whole tirade about it—and it was listening to the tirade that convinced me."

Pam was puzzled, so Bobby went on.

"You see, the more silly reasons he gave me why you shouldn't be working, the more I understood what *you* were going through trying to explain things to me!"

Pam burst out laughing. "Good old Jock! I'll have to tell him just how much I appreciate his help on this one!"

Pam and Bobby finished laughing and smiled warmly at each other. At last they had each other close again, she thought. They were home together, able to express their love again.

Bobby cocked his head and asked her, one last time, just for the reassurance he knew he'd hear:

"Pam, you won't let your job interfere with us, will you?" Then he gently took her hands in his.

Pam's brow wrinkled as she looked deeply into her husband's eyes.

"No! Never!" she said, meaning every word.

"But it's such a demanding job. How will you do it?"

"I'll do it! Somehow! *You* come first, Bobby. You always have and you always will!"

To prove her point, Pam gently drew Bobby to her and put her face tenderly on his cheek.

"I love you so much—so much . . ." she murmured, putting her arms around him.

The feel of her skin was warm and smooth. Bobby could feel himself melting.

"I love you, too," he whispered in her ear, thrilled by her closeness. And soon they had fallen back onto the bed to love each other as man and wife.

Chapter Twelve

Pam strolled onto the veranda wearing a low-cut green swimsuit. Today was the annual store inventory and the doors were closed to anyone but the clerks and the accountants. Her day off stretched before her, and she wanted to enjoy every minute of it. Ironically, those free hours meant so much more to her now, and she planned to use them far more productively than when she had been a "lady of leisure." Her project for today was reading from Charlotte Bronte's *Jane Eyre*. Pam had promised herself to read classics from world literature at least three times a year.

After an invigorating swim, filled with thoughts of warmth and love towards Bobby as she remembered their closeness the night before, she stepped out of the pool and toweled off with a thick Turkish towel embossed with the letter "E". Now she was ready to fall into the world of nineteenth century England by immersing herself in *Jane Eyre*.

She settled into a lounge chair, a pitcher of fresh

orangeade at her side, and opened the book to the place she had marked after the previous day's reading.

Jane Eyre had been awakened in the middle of the night by a strange piercing cry, as if from a wounded animal. But what could it be? Mr. Rochester, Jane's love, and owner of the grand estate where Jane had first come as a governess, was away in London. The only other occupants of the house were the housekeeper and her husband, two sour, dull souls. Jane looked to see if her bridal gown still lay on a chair in readiness for the wedding set for next week when Mr. Rochester would return. But now, the terrible shrieks were multiplying in a cacophony of horror as Jane began to smell smoke! The estate was on fire! Jane leaped from her bed and ran to the hallway where—

Just then, the telephone on the table next to Pam rang, piercing her concentration. Reluctant to be taken away from the drama of the book, Pam picked up the receiver still keeping her eyes on the page. A form was stalking Jane, an eerie form under a wedding veil—Jane's wedding veil. Closer it came and—

"Mrs. Ewing?" said the voice of a young girl at the other end.

"Ugh-uh" Pam murmured into the phone as Jane Eyre came face to face with a monstrous devil who—

"Mr. Connors called and he was wondering what hospital you want the baby born in. It don't matter to me much, long as I'm comfortable, and I figure since you're paying—"

As Pam's ears heard in spite of herself, she was

thrust back to Southfork with a jolt. Sue Ellen Ewing was buying herself a baby!

Pam's speech was muddled as she explained, "I'm sorry, I'm not Sue Ellen—" But before she could explain any further, the line at the other end was dead.

As she hung up, Pamela's mind was a rushing river filled with torrents of thought. How could Sue Ellen be planning to adopt a baby if J.R. knew nothing about it? What kind of situation was that for an innocent child to be thrust into? And J.R. would *never* allow it! *Never!* What was Sue Ellen letting herself in for?

There are times to interfere in the affairs of others, and times to stand back, Pam thought. But as she remembered the fear in Sue Ellen's eyes the last time they'd seen one another in town, her mind was made up. Poor Sue Ellen. So alone at a time when she most needed someone. How desperate her loneliness was that she would try to get a child this way. And did she fathom how serious a matter adoption was? That it would create a sea of emotions in the other people in the family? Could a woman who was afraid to address the Daughters of the Alamo be prepared to stand up against Jock and J.R. Ewing himself?

Walking to her sister-in-law's rooms, Pamela was determined to offer her friendship and support, even if that meant trying to talk her out of the adoption. Or, maybe Sue Ellen knew exactly what she was doing. In that case, Pam would be able to promise her support when the baby arrived and the Ewings realized what was going on.

Sue Ellen was busy packing Rita's overnight bag.

Brand new cosmetics, a cotton negligee, underwear, a vial of cologne and a toothbrush—everything a new mother would need to feel comfortable and attractive from her hospital bed. Rita's time could come soon and she wanted the girl to be prepared. That's why she assumed it was Teresa knocking lightly on her door. With J.R. at work, Bobby on the ranch, Miss Ellie in town at the DOA, and Pamela at work, there was nobody from the family at home. She opened the door without hesitation.

"Pamela!" was her horrified reaction.

"Hello, Sue Ellen. Mind if I come in and talk?"

"Well, I . . . I'm on my way to visit a friend. Uh, and I'm late actually, so . . ."

Pam looked behind her sister-in-law at the sea of suitcases and bathrobes and cosmetic cases and baby blankets on the bed. There was no doubt any more, and yet Sue Ellen was still trying to hide the obvious.

"Is this all for the Daughters of the Alamo, Sue Ellen?" Pam asked, showing a hint of annoyance at Sue Ellen's costly cloak-and-dagger approach to life. Why hadn't she just leveled with everyone and stood up for herself from the beginning! It would have made her life so much easier.

But then, Pam told herself, she shouldn't be so hard on Sue Ellen. The woman was married to J.R. Ewing—she could hardly be expected to be an emotionally healthy person after all!

"Sue Ellen—I came to say, you don't have to lie, not to me anyway. I mean, I have a pretty clear idea of what's going on and I just hope you know what you're doing."

Sue Ellen was silent, so Pam went on awkwardly.

"Maybe it would be a good thing to talk to someone about it—not me, necessarily, but—

Suddenly J.R.'s wife hissed like a cat at her sister-in-law. "How did you find out? How long have you been spying on me?"

"No! I never spied on you! Don't be silly, Sue Ellen. I would never do a thing like that. But, I just— I just put two and two together and I realized you're planning to take that girl's baby. But please, don't misunderstand, I don't want to interfere with any of your plans—I just thought you might need a friend, that's all. Someone to give you a little moral support or be a sounding board . . ."

"Well, if I wanted to talk to someone, the last person on earth I would choose is you! I hardly need advice from a shop girl about running my own life!"

Pam caught her breath. She could hardly believe that Sue Ellen was standing there, deliberately trying to hurt her. Why? Or did she just have so much pent-up anger and hurt in her that she would strike out against the first person to cross her path?

There was no use trying to be a good friend. Sue Ellen had made her anger and contempt clear. And maybe I *am* interfering, Pam thought. Maybe I should just back off and do what the Ewing family seems to spend so much time and energy doing whenever anything goes wrong—pretend everything is just fine, even when it isn't.

"I'm sorry Sue Ellen, I didn't mean to interfere. It's really none of my business anyway," Pam apologized with complete sincerity.

But Sue Ellen hardly heard her sister-in-law's gracious words. "And if you breathe a word of this to anyone I'll—I'll do something! I don't know what—but you won't get away with it!"

"I won't tell anyone, I promise."

"You better not."

Pam took one last look at Sue Ellen before she turned and left. Her sister-in-law looked pale, worried and frightened. But there was nothing Pam could do, so she said a perfunctory goodbye and left.

Breathing hard, Sue Ellen grabbed the overnight bag and flew down the stairs of Southfork. She had to see Rita. Rita was the only one who understood. Seeing Rita was like holding her baby. It was comforting. When she was with her, there was only the baby to think about, to dream about. There was nothing to hide, no charade to perform. Rita was her friend, Rita was the baby's reality. She had even told the girl that in the future she could come visit the child from time to time, as long as the child thought Sue Ellen was its true mother. She would introduce her as an "old, old friend of Mommy's." Sue Ellen knew that Buzz Connors disapproved of that kind of closeness between the adopting mother and the biological mother, but he didn't understand. He was a man after all, and men couldn't possibly know about friendship between women.

Sue Ellen swung open the door of Rita's apartment, but it was J.R.'s face that met hers.

"Hello, darlin'. I'm afraid you just missed your little friend."

His wife's eyes burned with anger as she pushed past him and flew into Rita's bedroom. The drawers were open, empty. There was not a piece of clothing in the closet.

Sue Ellen raced to the bathroom. A few hairpins

and a lipstick lying on the floor were the only remains of a hurried exit.

A cry burst out from deep inside her. "She's gone! Rita! My baby!" The word's were like a lonely wail into the wind.

She ran into the living room and shouted at J.R. "Monster! What did you do to her? What did you do to my baby?"

J.R. was unruffled and only slightly offended by Sue Ellen's shrieking and sobbing. There is nothing more unattractive than a hysterical woman, he thought.

"Calm down now, Sue Ellen. Your friend and her baby are safe and sound. In fact, they're on a bus right now to California. I took the liberty of giving her a bus ticket rather than plane fare since I thought she could use the extra money. I was more than generous, darlin', I assure you. What I gave her will keep her a year or more, if she has any brains at all— which she probably doesn't."

There was nothing she could say. Devastated, Sue Ellen rushed from the house. She had to get away from that emptiness!

Sue Ellen's car screeched in the Southfork driveway. On the patio, Jock, Ellie, Pam and Lucy were sipping cool drinks, enjoying the remainder of the sunny day. Sue Ellen burst onto the patio and headed straight for Pam, a look of hatred filling her face.

"You liar! You promised me! You swore you wouldn't tell him!" she yelled.

"Sue Ellen, please, what's the matter?" Ellie wanted to know as her two daughters-in-law stood frozen before each other.

"No! It's not true. I didn't tell anybody!" Pam cried out desperately.

"You did! He was there! He made her go!"

Jock and Ellie and Lucy looked at each other, uncomprehending.

"But you know something, Pam? You're lower than he is! He was right! You're nothing but a cheap hustler!"

"Now, just a minute, Sue Ellen!" Jock scolded in a deep firm tone.

But Sue Ellen went on, ignoring all but Pamela. "You'd do anything to usurp my position with this family! Well, you can have it! All of it! All the oil and all the money—the whole damned ranch and all the people on it! Because I don't want it anymore!"

And with that she stormed up to her room to pack.

The family looked at Pam speechlessly. Then J.R.'s car came skidding into the driveway. He tipped his hat gallantly as he passed through the stunned members of his family.

"Mama! Daddy! Lucy, Pam!" he said as he acknowledged each one with a slight movement. "Did Sue Ellen just get here?"

"Yes, son," was Jock's gruff answer.

"Well, then, if you'll excuse me—" and he hurried off after her.

The suitcases were out and already half full. Sue Ellen was working coolly and efficiently. For once in her life, she knew she was doing the right thing.

He watched her a minute incredulously, before he spoke. Finally, he said, quietly, "Now, darlin'. Let's not carry on so."

She kept packing with a vengeful energy as he stood still by the door.

"Sue Ellen? Darlin'? What are you doing?"

"What does it look like I'm doing, J.R.? I'm getting out! And I'm going far away from you and this place!"

She snapped the first suitcase shut and went to the closet for yet another.

"Now, honey," he said, "put that back. Nobody is going anywhere."

"Oh, yeah? Well, you're wrong, J.R.! You won't be able to buy your way out of this one!" was the reply she hissed.

J.R. walked very gingerly toward her as if she were a bomb primed to explode.

"But honey, I couldn't have you embarrass me in front of the family by doing such a silly thing as adopting a baby," he said as gently as he could.

For one agonized second, Sue Ellen stood still. Then, she opened her mouth and spoke the honest truth as she saw it. She owed him that.

"The reason I did what I did was that I thought a baby would help our marriage, J.R.—that's why I tried to get us a baby. But I know now, there's *no* help for you and me. *Nothing will help us!*"

J.R. walked closer. He had heard the crack of vulnerability in her voice and he knew she was a mass of jelly inside, no matter how hard her facade.

"But honey," he said smoothly, "you know I want a baby just as much as you do. I just want it to be *our* baby. I don't want anyone else's—only our very own dear little child."

"Well, isn't that nice of you, J.R.!" she retorted sarcastically, wiping away the hint of tears in her eyes. "But how are we supposed to get our dear little child—through witchcraft? You never even look at me, let alone touch me! I practically have to beg you every time, and half the time you shoo me away!"

J.R. was close enough now to reach out to her. But when she felt the touch of his hands on her shoulders, she hit him hard across the face. He grabbed her closer and squeezed her arms tightly.

"I told you never to do that!" he warned.

"Just let me go!" she cried, struggling with all her might to release herself from his grip. The feel of his skin on hers sent a sick chill through her.

"Don't touch me!" she cried.

"Why not?" he asked. "You're my wife. I'm allowed."

"Oh, no you're not! Not if I don't want it! And I don't!"

"You want me, darlin'. You've been wanting me like crazy. I've noticed all those sheer nightgowns and what not you've been parading in, hoping you would get some attention from me. You were acting like a cheap floozy, Sue Ellen, that's how bad you wanted me. Well, I'm not going to deny you any more. Now is your chance. I'm going to give you what you really want—what you've always wanted from me!"

He was kissing her now, his lips covering her mouth like a vacuum. Sue Ellen felt a wave of nausea.

"Let me go! Let me go!" she struggled to say, but the words couldn't escape. She felt herself being pushed back on the bed.

"You animal!" she finally gasped.

"You have no say about it, darlin'. You lost your vote," she heard him murmur . . .

The morning was full of incredible brightness as the sun drifted high above in a cotton candy sky.

Breakfast done, Pam and Bobby were laughing as he led her by the hand down the front steps of the mansion.

"Keep your eyes shut now!" he ordered, as they made their way to the driveway.

"Come on, Bobby! You can just tell me what it is, you know!" she pleaded happily, her eyes tightly closed.

"No! Keep 'em shut! Two more steps—Okay! Open them!"

A brand new black Corvette, complete with a giant red ribbon, greeted Pam Ewing's eyes.

"Oh, Bobby!" she cried in surprise.

"I mean, if you've got a job, you need a car, right? Couldn't have you keep borrowing mine!" he laughed.

Pam fell into her husband's welcoming arms as the lovers kissed each other warmly. Then the door to the mansion opened. It was Sue Ellen.

"Sue Ellen!" Pam called. "Excuse me, Bobby."

Sue Ellen was perfectly coifed and stylishly dressed as she stood frozen on the mansion steps.

"I didn't want to say anything at breakfast, but I hope you know I didn't tell, Sue Ellen," Pam said, afraid of the response she might get.

But Sue Ellen's eyes betrayed nothing as she answered calmly, her voice devoid of emotion. "Of course. I was just very upset yesterday. And I'm very sorry I yelled at you like that, Pam."

"Well, don't worry about me—but, are you okay?"

Sue Ellen smiled her best Miss Texas smile.

"Oh, I'm just fine, Pam. In fact, J.R. and I have decided that we'd rather have a baby of our own than adopt one anyway."

Bobby was now in the Corvette, tooting its horn. "Come on, Pam! Don't you want to take a ride before work?"

Pam turned toward her husband. "Yes! I'm coming!" she called out as she turned from the steps and hurried to her new car.

Just then, J.R. appeared in the doorway next to his wife and waved to his brother and sister-in-law as they drove away. "Y'all have a good day now!"

And putting his arm around his wife's unresponsive body, he cheerfully noted, "Bobby bought his bride a little toy, I see."

Sue Ellen stood as still as a mummy.

"Well," he continued, as if she had answered, "anything you'll be needing in town today, darlin'?"

This time she answered. "No."

It was the one word she would speak to him again. Last night had convinced her once and for all. Her marriage to J.R. was finished. But there would be no divorce. She didn't want it and neither did he. There was no reason to walk away from the family fortune by leaving him. The shell of the marriage would still exist for all the world to see, but the heart and soul of it was forever gone.

She would live as he lived, finding love where she could, meeting her physical needs as she wanted to. She was free of him now in every way.

Maybe someday there would be a child in her life,

somehow. And maybe everything would work out for the best. But one thing was certain, she was no longer chained to J.R. No matter what he did, he couldn't hurt her any more.

"Well, then, darlin', I guess I'll be off," he was saying, bussing her cheerfully on the cheek as a loving husband would do.

"Oh, and sweetheart," he called to her as she turned to go back in the house, "I have a little business meeting in town and I probably won't be home till very late tonight. No need to wait up for me."

Sue Ellen opened the door without acknowledging she had heard him. She would never wait up for him again!

YOU CAN NOW ORDER PREVIOUS
TITLES OF SOAPS & SERIALS™ BOOKS
BY MAIL

Just complete the order form and detach on the dotted line and send together with your check or money order payable to **SOAPS & SERIALS**:

SOAPS & SERIALS™
120 Brighton Road, Box 5201
Clifton, NJ 07015-5201

Please circle the books you wish to order:

THE YOUNG AND THE RESTLESS	BK #	1 2 3
DAYS OF OUR LIVES		1 2 3
GUIDING LIGHT		1 2 3
ANOTHER WORLD		1 2 3
AS THE WORLD TURNS		1 2 3
CAPITOL™		1 2 3
DALLAS™		1 2 3
KNOTS LANDING™		1 2 3

Each book is $2.50 ($3.25 in Canada).

Total number of books circled _____
  @ $2.50   ($3.25 Canada) $_____
Sales tax (CT residents only) $_____
Shipping and Handling $_____.95
Total payment enclosed (checks or
  money orders only) $_____
Name _____
Address _____ **Apt. #** _____
City _____
State _____ **Zip** _____
Telephone No. _____

D3